FOUR LETTER WORDS

Michael Stewart

Also by Michael Stewart

King Crow
Café Assassin
Mr Jolly
Couples
Ill Will
Walking the Invisible

"Modern fiction at its innovative best."
Melvin Burgess

"Beautifully ammoniacal and intense."
Will Self

"One of the best novels I have read in years."
David Peace

"Dark, funny and twisted."
A.L. Kennedy

"Bleak but wonderful."
Alan Bennett

"As good as British fiction gets."
Loud and Quiet

FOUR LETTER WORDS

Michael Stewart

All rights reserved. No part of this book may be reproduced, stored in a retrieval system or transmitted in any form or by any means electronic, mechanical, photocopying, recording or otherwise, without the prior permission of the publisher.

ISBN 978-1903110898

First published in this edition 2022 by Wrecking Ball Press

Copyright © Michael Stewart

Book design: humandesign.co.uk

All rights reserved.

For the lost and the lonely

'when a woman says no' was the winner of the *H.E. Bates Short Story Prize 2019;* 'painting the walls white' was first published in *High Spirits: A Round of Drinking Stories,* ed. Karen Stevens and Jonathan Taylor (Valley Press); 'as many grains of sand' was first published by *Galley Beggar Press* as an e-book.

WORK/

1. when a woman says no 17
2. painting the walls white 23
3. a black sheep in the white swan 31
4. as many grains of sand 35
5. just a job 43
6. baby snakes 47
7. a four letter word 55

HOME/

1. just waving 85
2. home 91
3. the shivering man 93
4. a better devil 105
5. henry the hoover 109
6. between the lights 113

WORK

"If you liked school, you'll love work." Irvine Welsh

16

when a woman says no

There's always something to do if you put your mind to it. You are wiping down the tops and polishing the taps when the landlord stands at the end of the bar, scratching his beard. As he scratches, he stares at you, his eyes tracing your outline. He does this when it's quiet. He has CCTV cameras pointing at you and he watches on the screens upstairs. He waits until the pub is almost empty then he comes down and leans against the panelled counter. You keep yourself busy, emptying the glass cleaner, stacking the shelves, cleaning the pumps. The fire could do with a stoke. You walk across and give it a prod with the poker. You take the coal scuttle and chuck on some more fuel. It's cheap stuff. The landlord gets it off one of the regulars. Too much slag to sell commercially. It's a pain to burn. It doesn't give out that much heat and it forms a crust that stops air getting in, so you have to keep an eye on it and routinely poke through the crust. As you bend over to pour the coal in, you can feel his eyes all over you.

The landlord has been sending you pictures of his cock. The first time you thought it was a mistake. He lives upstairs with his wife, Emma. They have three young lads. Maybe he meant to send it to Emma. So you ignored it. Only, about a week later, you got another one. No words. No explanation. Just a picture of his cock. Why do men do that? Why do they think you want to see pictures of their cocks? If anything it puts you off. You've come across it before. On dating sites. Women send pictures of their faces. Smiling or pouting. But some blokes just send you blurry photos of their cocks. Hard and soft. Suppose they want you to send something back. Like a dare. A provocation. You ignored that one as well.

Four days later he sends the third photo. You thought about replying, no thanks, I don't like molluscs. But would he even know what molluscs are? He isn't very bright. Just enough intelligence to run a bar and he doesn't even do that very well. Always letting the beer go off or forgetting to order enough stock. Anyway, a reply might encourage him. Even, fuck off, or, do one. Always best to ignore. That's always the thing to do.

Now, here he is, leaning against the bar, staring at you. It's a Tuesday afternoon. There's another bloke at the opposite end of the counter. A regular. Uses a walking stick. He looks to be in his seventies but you know for a fact he is only fifty-four. He's no real harm. Stands there all day drinking pints of cider. Every half hour or so he staggers outside to smoke a fag. Sometimes he tries to talk to you. It's hard to tell what he is saying, so you just nod, or smile, or laugh. You wonder if he's had a stroke, or whether it is the result of years of hard drinking. Another bloke sits by the window. His name is Raymond. He's there at eleven every morning when the doors are opened. His wife has died and his daughter is living in New Zealand. He drinks twenty pints a day and never seems to get drunk. You wonder where he gets his money from. He hasn't worked for years. There's an old woman sitting opposite him, sipping that nasty wine the landlord sells on draught. She sits on her own. Does the Sudoku, then the quick crossword. Sometimes she asks for help, but you've never been any good at puzzles. She drinks four or five large wines then stumbles home. You can't remember the old lady's name. No one can. Mavis or Doris, or something like that. They are what is left of the pub industry. Relics of another world. Just waiting for the reaper. Each drink is an invitation.

Raymond stands up and walks over to the bar. Same again. Cheers, love. You hold his glass under the tap but all that comes out is a trickle. Like an old man's piddle. I'll have to change the barrel, you say. No bother, love. Not going nowhere. Take your time. You put the glass down and walk over to the steps at the back of the bar, into the cellar.

It's dark down there, even with the light on. Just one bulb covered in cobwebs and filth. It takes a while for your eyes to adjust. You go over to where the lager kegs are stored. You unscrew the coupling from the top of the empty keg and attach it to a full one. You hear footsteps and look over to the doorway. It's the landlord. He looks over, nods sternly, then closes the door behind him. He bolts it. He walks over to you, working his way past barrels and kegs, crates of beer and soft drinks, until he gets up close. It's only a small cellar and there isn't much space between the kegs and crates and barrels. He is almost touching you. You can feel his beard on your neck and he whispers, I want to feel your tits.

You try to keep your cool. You return his gaze. He strokes his beard softly and stares down at your chest. The silence is thick, just the hum of the air conditioning unit. You see a spider scurry over the bare bulb. At last you say, Fuck off, and push him out of the way. You unbolt the door and go back up to the bar.

That night, when you get home, your dad asks how work has gone. Ok. Was it busy? No, just the usual. You put a couple of pizzas in the oven and make a fresh pot of tea. After you've eaten your dad says, everything alright? Yeah, why? Just, you've not said two words. Not like you. Someone upset you? No, just tired. Think I'm going to hit the sack, Dad. You kiss him on his forehead and leave him watching some crap on telly.

You try to get to sleep, but your mind is playing the scene over and over again. I want to feel your tits. I want to feel your tits. Not even, can I feel your tits? It's like he just expects you to get them out and let him do what he wants. And Emma in the room above looking after his three kids. Maybe you should tell her. Doesn't she deserve to know? Would she believe you? You don't really get on with Emma. You've tried in the past. Maybe Emma sees you as competition. You are sure you're not the only barmaid he's tried it on with. He's been with Emma four years. Emma had been a barmaid at the time they got together and he was with a woman called Rachel. So Emma knows the score. Knows what her bloke is like. Better than anyone. Just as you are drifting off to sleep, your phone pings. It's a text from the landlord. It says, when a woman says no, she usually means, yes. You ignore it, set your alarm, turn the volume to mute and plug in the charger.

The next day is another quiet shift. The pub is empty most of the time. The quiz night's popular on a Tuesday. Thursday nights bring in a few folk musicians who have a jam. They aren't big drinkers though, nursing one pint each the whole evening. Fridays and Saturdays are busy and Sunday afternoons. Not much Monday to Wednesday. Nothing much at night and even less during the day. You often wonder how long the pub can go on for. And in the winter, it takes so much wood and coal just to keep the place from freezing. Sometimes it's even quiet at weekends. Occasionally the landlord puts a band on Saturday night, but it isn't a regular slot and it's hit and miss if there's an audience or not. He's too tight to pay for a band that would pack the place out.

You are filling up the fridges when you see the landlord standing at the bar. He scratches his beard, then strokes it softly, all the time staring at you. Then he lifts up the hatch and walks over to you. Pretending not to notice him, you take another beer bottle out of the crate and line it up on the fridge shelf, turning it so that the label is facing out.

He leans down and whispers in your ear, Have you still got those photos on your phone? You don't look at him, take another bottle and stack it on the shelf. You say in a low voice, My phone is a grenade. He doesn't say anything but you see the fear in his eyes. He nods, then goes back upstairs to his wife and kids. You chuckle to yourself. It is one of those random things. You hadn't meant to say it. You think about it. You could get some posters made, stick them up outside the pub. Pictures of his cock with some text maybe. Something simple like, This is the landlord's cock. Come inside for a warm welcome. But on the bus on the way home you are shaking. Is it rage? Is it? What is it?

When you get home your dad says, You alright, love? You close the door, lock it, take the key out and put it in the bowl, then burst into tears. He wants to know what's wrong, but you can't tell him. He puts his arms round you and gives you a hug. Now, now, calm yourself, it can't be all bad. He sits you down and puts the kettle on, but all you can tell him is that you've had a bad day at work. Has a customer upset you? No, it's not that. Well, what is it? You just shake your head. Doesn't matter. It's dealt with. You sure? You nod. The last thing you want is your dad kicking off. He'll go round there and have it out with him. Might even smack him one. And you don't want your dad fighting your battles. You are twenty-seven years old. For fuck sake.

You watch telly with your dad for a bit. Then you kiss him good night and climb up the stairs. You're not working tomorrow. Day off. But you're working Friday and Saturday. You'll have it out with him then. Threaten to tell Emma. See how he likes that. You lie back in your bed and close your eyes but as you do you hear his words in your head. When a woman says, no, she usually means yes. Was it meant to be a joke? Does he believe that?

Friday is a busy shift. Just how you like it. It's the end of the week and people just want to unwind. A good atmosphere, loud but not aggressive. The shift whizzes by and before you know it you're calling last orders. You saw the landlord earlier on but he's disappeared upstairs again. He doesn't spend that much time in the pub, and when he does he's usually with his mates, pissed. He prefers to be upstairs where he can watch the bar on CCTV.

Folk scramble to the pumps, eager to get one for the road. You are kept busy as you try to serve them all. Then you're ushering them out. Just two stragglers. Two young lads who can't take their ale. You steer them out of the front door and bolt it behind them. You've already taken off the sprinklers and put them in a glass of soda water. Just need to lock up. You go into the kitchen to fetch your coat and scarf, freezing outside. The landlord is standing by the fridge with the door open. His beard is illuminated by the fridge light.

Just grabbing some supper. Do you want anything? Got some pork pies left.

No. I'm done. I've got some supper at home. Best be off.

Don't go. Not yet. I wanted to talk to you about something.

Not now, I'm too tired. Besides, there's a taxi waiting for me outside. Tell me tomorrow.

You walk past him, grabbing your coat and scarf off the hook as you turn to leave.

Listen, that text I sent.

What about it?

It was a joke. You know that?

Yeah, course it was. I'm not daft.

He nods and strokes his beard.

I was pissed. Just a joke, right?

Yeah, you say, as you zip up your coat and wrap your scarf round your neck. I'll see you tomorrow.

In the taxi, you go over the incident in your head. Should have come out with it. Told him to pack it in.

Listen, if you do anything like that again. I've kept the photos. You say another word. I'll tell Emma. I'll show her the texts. You see if I don't. Just try it. I dare you.

You pay the driver. Grab a take-away from the shop at the end of the street. Fumble with your key. Just me, you say, as you close the door, lock it and bolt it. I've got fish and chips for supper. Do you want some?

That would be grand, your dad says. I'll put the kettle on.

You both sit on the sofa watching whatever your dad has been watching. It's a film. You see a babysitter put a child to bed, tuck them in, and walk down some stairs. The bulb flickers. The babysitter is about to sit down when she hears something outside and peers through the window. She can't see anything. Too dark. She goes into the living room and is about to sit down again when she hears something outside once more. She goes to the patio door and peers again. Nothing. She opens the door and walks outside, into the engulfing darkness.

Why do they always do that? your dad says. Doesn't make any sense, does it? In real life you keep the door shut. You don't open it. You walk away from trouble, not towards it. Pass us some more chips.

You tip some onto his plate. Salt and vinegar? You sip hot tea from your mug, holding it with both hands, pressing it against your chest. You feel its warmth. Maybe you should get another job? But there aren't that many decent bar jobs these days. Most of the pubs have closed. Besides, all the landlords are the same. Who's to say the next one won't try it on? Better stick to what you know. At least you know where you are. At least you know what he's like. Your dad is chewing chips and slurping his drink. On the telly it is dark. All you can hear is a woman screaming, out of shot.

painting the walls white

When Will Brotherton was sacked from FS Solutions he saw it as a door opening. But his wife, Kate, was pissed off. What was he going to do now? He told her that he'd always wanted to work for himself. He'd always dreamed about becoming a self-employed painter and decorator. Kate was sceptical, but the next day he went down to Northway Vans and bought a ten-year-old Berlingo. He put an advert in the community magazine and stuck a card in the post office window. He went to the pub and put the word around. Nothing.

Two weeks passed by before the phone rang. A Mrs Barker wanted her window frames painting before the weather turned. He went to the address she had given him and he counted the windows.

How much? Mrs Barker asked.

He had some idea of the cost of paint, having decorated his daughter's bedroom a few months ago. The window frames would need sanding and priming first, then undercoating, with two coats of gloss to finish. He gave Mrs Barker a price.

The job took the best part of three days. The weather was dry and the sky wasn't too cloudy. It was good to work outside with the sun on his skin. He listened to his portable radio and hummed along to the music. There was something very satisfying about painting over the drab paint with a shiny new coat. He was taking something old and rejuvenating it. It felt like a kind of rebirth.

The old woman was happy with the job and paid him in cash. He went to the pub and bought a pint. He sat outside and watched the wind rustle the leaves. This was the life. He was his own boss. He could do what he liked now.

The old woman had told her friends and within a few weeks he was booked up solid. He stopped arguing with Kate. She accepted his new business and was even proud of him. For the first time in months they made love. The work kept coming in and he had to turn people down. He thought about taking someone else on.

But then, as winter came and Christmas approached, the work dried up. No one wanted the decorators in at Christmas. He was sure it would pick up again in the New Year.

January, though, was as dead as December. He still had a bit of cash left over and he liked spending more time with his daughter. He took her to the park, or, if it was raining, to an indoor play centre with a ball pool. It was good to see her run around with the other kids.

When February came, only a few jobs trickled in and he started to fret. What if he'd made a terrible mistake? Would he have to go back to Mr Barnett with his tail between his legs and beg for his old job back? The thought chilled him. At night, Kate turned away from him in bed.

Will felt immense relief when he got a phone call from the manager of a warehouse company.

The next day he drove out of town to a new industrial estate next to a motorway. The building was huge, easily the biggest unit on the estate. He rang the bell and was ushered into the waiting area. Five minutes later he was shown around by the manager: a neat man of average height, not much older than Will. He led him into the main room which was like an aircraft hangar. It was completely empty. The man explained that they were going to fill it with stock soon, but wanted to get it painted first. Was he interested?

Will looked around. It was a massive job and it would take him weeks and weeks to paint it: he wouldn't have to worry about money for at least two months.

Yes, I can do it. What colour?

White.

It was white already and it didn't really look in need of another coat, but Will kept this thought to himself.

No problem, he said.

White's the cheapest colour, he thought.

Will gave the man a price that he'd inflated quite a bit. He'd need a break after painting this, he thought. The man seemed happy and they shook on it. When Will got home that night, Kate was delighted.

He's got some more warehouses a bit further out, so if I make a good job of this, he said he'd give me those to do as well.

That's brilliant, said Kate. And she gave him a big smile. That night in bed, she let him cup one of her breasts.

The next day he bought the paint and made his way to the warehouse. The secretary gave him his own key. She said they were only there some of the time, so he'd have to let himself in. She showed him where everything was and then left him to it. He brought some sheets in from the van but realised he wouldn't need them. There was nothing to splash. He had bought extra-large rollers with an extension arm so he could reach the tops of the walls from his ladder. He opened a fresh tub of white paint and poured a generous amount into a black tray. He dipped in the roller, squeezed out the excess paint, and began to paint the white walls white.

It was easy at first, but as he worked it became more difficult to decide where he had painted. He thought of a system. He would paint left to right, starting at the bottom and working his way up. But still, after an hour of this, he kept forgetting where he had got to. You had to catch the wet paint with the light on it because it reflected the light better than dry paint. After another hour his eyes started playing tricks on him. The white was straining his eyes and he could no longer tell which was wet and which was dry paint. He came up with another plan. He took out a pencil and marked up a portion of the wall, then he took a section and marked it up into squares. This way he could easily tell where he had got to.

He grafted till past one o'clock, then sat down in a corner on the unused dust sheets and ate his sandwiches. He poured himself coffee from his flask

25

and listened to the radio. He surveyed his progress. He'd been working for over four hours and he had hardly made a dent in it. The wall was vast and he'd only painted about three or four percent. He'd be lucky to have finished ten percent by the end of the day. Ten days to paint that one wall, and then there were three others. Forty days. That was well within his estimate of fifty days. If he kept at it, at the same rate, he'd be able to take a few days off before the next job. Another warehouse the same size as this one. Also painted white.

On the drive home, all he could see were white walls. All he could smell was the tang of white paint.

He was very quiet that night when he and Kate sat down for their evening meal.

Are you ok? she asked.

Fine.

He went to bed early and dreamed he was painting a white wall white. When he stepped back, he could not see where the wall started or where it ended. He woke up and stared at the clock. It was 5am. He lay back again but couldn't sleep. All he could think about were white walls. Endless white walls.

That day he worked hard, trying to shake off the dream. He turned up the radio and sang along to the music at the top of his voice. First 'Money, Money, Money', then 'Should I Stay Or Should I Go?'. His voice echoed in the empty chamber.

After work, he called into his local pub and had a pint.

Where have you been?

He explained that painting walls was thirsty work. Kate didn't seem to mind that much. The next evening he stopped for two pints and she commented again. He apologised. But a pattern soon formed: calling in for a skinful on the way home; arguing with Kate when he got back. At night he'd have the same dream, in which he'd wake up inside a white cube with no way in or out. Then he'd wake up again.

In the warehouse, no matter how loud he played the radio, he couldn't concentrate. He tried to sing along to the music but the words would blur and the white walls would undulate in front of his eyes. He stared into the tubs of white paint and recalled the bottomless well in a story he'd read as a kid. It had always terrified him. He imagined falling into the endless whiteness.

That night they argued.

How many have you had? she said.

I don't know, I don't keep count, he slurred.

You'll get stopped by the police.

He shrugged.

Or worse. You'll end up killing someone. Is that what you want?

He shrugged again.

You're drinking away the profits, Will. What's the point in that?

I don't give a fuck!

You don't give a fuck about us then, do you? You don't give a fuck about your daughter. You don't give a fuck about me.

He lowered his voice, Look, Kate, I don't think I can do it anymore.

What do you mean?

The job. I don't think I can finish it.

Why not? It's easy enough, isn't it? It's good money. You're your own boss. Isn't that what you wanted?

He was being unreasonable, in her eyes. He'd been sacked from a perfectly good job once more, but had set up his own business. Now he'd made a success of it. He'd secured a big contract, giving him months and months of steady work.

He went to bed early that night. She put her hand on his shoulder when she came to bed later, but he pretended to be asleep.

The next day he drove out to the warehouse and gave himself a good talking to. Come on, Will, man-up. You can do this. It's not like you're working down a mine or working outside in the middle of winter. It's not the Somme. It's easy work. No heavy lifting. No danger.

He turned the radio on and opened a tub of fresh paint. He marked off the sections he planned to do that day and got cracking. He was working on the top parts of the wall and had to fully extend the ladder to get into the corners. The ladder started to wobble. He took it easy. The concrete floor was a long way down. He'd smash his bones to pieces if he lost his balance.

27

But as he stared at the white wall, at the old dry white paint and the new wet white paint, he felt himself becoming disorientated. Which way was up and which way was down? The ladder was shaking. He tried to keep as still as possible, but the ladder kept on shaking. He looked down. Yes, that was down. And it was a long way. He would break his back or his neck if he fell. The ground seemed to disappear beneath him. He was falling into the well and there was nothing to hold on to as the white walls rushed past, the whiteness engulfing him.

Eventually the ladder stopped shaking and he slowly climbed back down. He lay on the floor and stared at the white ceiling and the white walls. He was surrounded by white. Imprisoned by it. This was hell. Not fire and brimstone, just a huge cube of whiteness. He couldn't see beyond it. He didn't know how he was ever going to get past it.

A pint of lager and a whiskey chaser.

It wasn't even three o'clock but he was done for the day. He sat in a corner, necked the whiskey in one and gulped down the lager. He went back to the bar and reordered, necking the drinks once more. He tried to get the image of the white walls out of his mind. The vast cube of white all around him. Something was on the telly in the other corner of the pub, but he couldn't make any sense of it. There were a few other people in the pub now. Solo drinkers. Workers clocking off early, or people on benefits. He bought another round.

It was eight o'clock already. He should be going home. Kate would be wondering where he was. She'd be worried about him. He went to the bar and ordered one more for the road. When he tried to pay the barmaid, his change spilled over the floor. Coins rolled under tables and chairs. He stared at them, incapable of picking them up. The room was spinning. He clung to the bar and took out a ten-pound note.

Are you ok? the barmaid said as she took the note. He sat back down in the corner with his drinks. There were more people in now. Or was he seeing double? The room was moving. He kept forgetting where he was. Good, that was the idea: he wanted to forget where he was and who he was.

It was gone nine when he came round to the barmaid shaking his arm.

You can't behave like this in here, she said. You'll have to go home.

She was staring down on him with a look of horror. He looked back at her uncomprehending.

You've had enough, she said. You're disturbing the other customers.

A pint glass was smashed on the table in front.

Don't come back. You're barred.

He woke up at the bottom of the stairs, fully dressed. His head was banging. He stumbled to his feet. Outside his van was parked at an angle to the road. There was a dent in one of the panels. His wife had left a note: *we need to talk.*

After a cold shower, he set off for work but found himself pulling into a different pub. All day he sat there drinking. Other drinkers were chatting at the bar. A couple close by were holding hands. He watched the local news on the plasma screen. The weatherman was issuing a weather warning. A cold snap was due from the east. He stared at the glass in front and raised it to his lips. He remembered when Kate had first held his hand. They had met in a pub. She was friends with someone from work who introduced them. They said hello but they were both a bit shy. He'd got her number and they'd arranged to meet in a bar a few days later. Conversation had been awkward at first, but they found they had a lot in common and soon she was smiling and laughing at his jokes. It was towards the end of the night. He was walking out with her and it had just happened. Her hand in his, like a miracle.

Outside, the cold night air sobered him up a little. It was snowing and must have been snowing for hours. For once the weather forecast had been right. Where had he parked the van? All the vehicles were covered. He meandered across the car park, searching for his Berlingo. But it was no use. The cars all looked the same covered in snow. He walked in between vehicles and further across the car park, traipsing through a crisp flurry which crunched under his boots. As he did he tripped and fell. The security lighting shone around him and as he lay back in the snow, he was surrounded by whiteness. He stared at the sky, now filled with tumbling snowflakes. He watched them fall and felt them land on his body and face.

Thick cold white blobs. At first cold, until his skin numbed. He couldn't see out of his eyes. He could feel his blood cooling and his heart slowing. Busy at the bar now. Hardly move. Had his beer gone? There was Kate, holding his hand, like she did on their first date. Her hand was warm and smooth. And the night wasn't over. She was enjoying herself too much to go home. Did he know a bar they could go to for a final drink? He knew just the place, where they could get one last beer and whiskey chaser. One for the road.

a black sheep in the white swan

Spare any change, mate? You know like bloke just walks past dunt even look. Never do. Except. Now. And. Again. Not bad work. Get a few bob. Don't know. I do daft things me. Not right in the head like. You wouldn't think but. When I had my flat I had a bit more of a clue. Like. When I was on the dole I had this idea. I was walking past a house. Bloke up on the roof fixing his aerial. And I thought, nice ladder. Then I thought, I could use that. It didn't occur to me till I'd got the ladder back to mine, that I'd left him up there, with a TV aerial in one hand and a screwdriver in the other. What I did like was go round to people's houses and knock on their door. Ask them if they wanted their gutters cleaning. Twenty quid a go. I dint knock on everyone's door. I looked first, made sure there were weeds and that poking out. Sometimes I'd nip up beforehand like, put some weeds up there myself. You've got to like use your initiative ant yer. I made a few bob. Only one day I knocked on this door and the door was open but there were no one there. So

Spare any change, mate? I need. Not a bad spot this for a bit of work normally do alright. Not today, like. Well, yer know what I mean like. I was brought up in the seventies. And for some reason, in the seventies, you were made to believe, if you went round people's houses during the day, like as a window cleaner or something or anything really that there were like loads of bored housewives hanging about in like see-through negligees and that just gagging for a shag. I did make a few bob. Only one day I fell off. That's when I developed vertigo. Next day when I went up the ladder I looked down and my head started to spin. The cracks in the flagstones kept jolting right in front of me, like they were cracks in a pair of glasses I was wearing. Which is

Spare any change, mate? Got back from London yesterday. Skipped the train. Spent an hour in the toilet, hiding from the conductor. Stunk of shit. Someone kept knocking on the door. You finished in there? You finished? But I just groaned and he went away. Came out after. Found a place to sit. One of them free papers. I'm trying to read it. The durr-dumm durr-dumm of the train as its wheels go over the track.

Don't suppose you've got a fag have you, mate? Or some tobacco? I'm gagging. I'm sat in one of those chairs like where there's a table. I'm travelling backwards. I don't like that. This woman sits opposite and straight away she's on her phone. Then this lad who's sat next to me, like right snotty little teenager with his mum and dad. They're a bit posh and he's obviously in his like rebel stage because he's got a pierced eyebrow and like a Rancid T-shirt on. He's fishing about in his rucksack. Gets out his phone and fiddles about with it. The music starts and he shakes his head. And I think, fuck this. All I hear is the muffled drums and the distorted bass. But over the top I can just make out the lyrics, Burn motherfuckers, burn! And I think, I could really do with a fag. They used to let you smoke on the train. Now they don't let you do owt. The only other time I was on a train though was back when you could smoke. I fucked it up. They asked me whether I wanted smoking or non-smoking, and like a fucking dick, I said non-smoking. Cos I thought like, yeah I'm an addict, but that's too much like tempting fate. You buy a ticket that says smoking on it and you're asking for like trouble if you see what I mean. I've got a thing about trains. Well not about trains so much, more like about the train crash like. You know Hatfield, Ladbroke Grove, all that. So I didn't want to push it. I didn't want to like make the train crash. If you think about it hard enough you can. Then this ring tone, the Birdie Song, you can now like buy the Birdie Song as a ring tone, like who the fuck would want to do that unless you want to like piss people off? I'm looking round me and I'm hot and I'm sweating and one of my headaches starts. Like an axe, right through mi fucking head. And the durr-dumm, durr-dumm is making it worse, and she's still on her phone, really? Really? Really? And the drum and the bass, flat and distorted. Reallyreallyreally. And I'm going backwards, like I'm getting sucked into this vortex, with a blur of trees and verges, blues and greens streaming either side of me – whoosh, whoosh. And I want to scream. Whoosh. Whoosh. Really. Really. Durr-dumm. Durr-dumm. I want to explode. And I look up and I see this emergency hammer. And it says, in case of emergency, break glass. And I'm thinking like, this is an emergency. I'm thinking, this is a fucking crisis. But I'm thinking, the emergency hammer like is behind the glass right. So I like need an emergency hammer to get the emergency hammer. Who thought that one up? Like fucked up or what. How like fucked up is that? And you wonder why the trains are fucked. You wonder why it's all fucked. It's

Got enough for a cup of tea, mate? You know, I'm spitting feathers. Can't hardly swallow. But I liked that hammer. I would have liked to have had that hammer. Like a trophy, like a prize medal. I'd have it mounted like on a plinth. Put it on my mantelpiece. Keep it there. Just for like emergencies.

I saw her yesterday.
She said she didn't love me anymore.
She said, she felt like I was weighing her down.
She was with him. I don't blame her like. But I said to her, It's best we stay mates. For the sake of the kids like. Fuck that, she said, I don't want Ryan and Zoe to grow up with a thief for a dad. Best if I stay away and never make contact. I got all choked up. It's fucking pathetic like, but I started to blubber like a big kid. She said, It's best if yer go. So I went to the White Swan. And it's nice. And it's sunny. I buy a pint of Black Sheep, and I go and sit outside by the water. There was this girl, bout the same age as Zoe. And she was picking some blossom. She stands on the railings by the side of the river with this blossom. Wonderful it was, frothy, like foam, and she

starts throwing it into the water. And it travels through the air so soft and so slow, like falling is the most gentle thing in the world. And it hits the water without making a sound. And then it drifts down the river. I looked at that girl. Not a care in the world. And I don't know what happened I don't know why I did it but the next thing I'm walking off with her hand in hand I get round the corner Where's my mummy? I want my mummy. Shut up just shut up right. Shut it. And I'm running and dragging her behind me. She's crying. Mum. Mummy. Mum. I let go of her just leg it as fast as I can till I'm a mile away. And I stop to get my breath. And I just don't know why I did it. I can't think

Spare any change, mate? Jus

as many grains of sand

I first met David at a work function. We were in a rather expensive bar in the centre of town and my line manager, Merrick, introduced us. We shook hands and David offered to buy me a drink. We found a cosy corner and sat down. I immediately felt at ease in his presence: his eyes sparkled and his smile was warm. David was of average height and build. He wore a black suit with a grey open-necked shirt. His hair was dark and combed back. He wore a gold wedding ring, but no other adornments. As he reached for his cocktail glass, I noticed that his hands were finely manicured. He looked good for a man in his late fifties.

So, how are you adjusting to the new role? he said.

It was one of those questions that could come across as insincere, but he smiled at me in such a genuine way, that I knew he really wanted to know.

Well, I'm still learning the ropes, I said. I'm getting the hang of it though.

He's doing a brilliant Job, Merrick said, and gave me a wink.

David told me how pleased they were with my progress and I felt myself grow. He regretted that he hadn't been there at my interview. He'd been away on business.

I'd been promoted to head of sales only three weeks previously and rewarded with my own office, a company car, six weeks annual leave and a big pay rise. I was on good money and my wife and I were looking to move to a bigger house in the country. She wanted a hot tub in the garden. It felt like a bit of a gimmick to me, one of those things you use a few times until the novelty wears off, but I humoured her. We could easily afford it now. She was on good money too. Working for an airline.

We chatted for a while and David outlined his vision for the company. He had big plans for expansion and he wanted me to contribute.

Let's get together next week, he said. Do a bit of brainstorming.

We didn't stay long. I was driving Merrick home, so I couldn't have more than two drinks. We said our goodbyes and I shook hands with David again. It was such a warm and reassuring handshake.

It's been great to meet you, he said. You're my kind of guy. And we laughed.

We were both quiet on the drive home. Merrick had drunk more than me and he seemed a bit tired. He was content to sit back and listen to the radio. It was dark outside and the headlights formed two white eyes in the road. Merrick lived out in the sticks. Some of the roads were single track and I was concentrating, driving cautiously, my right foot hovering over the brake, even though there was no other traffic. Eventually Merrick turned to me and said, So, what do you think of David?

First impressions? He seems really nice. I mean, not like a boss of a big company. Do you know what I mean? He just seems really laid back and friendly. There's no edge. I took to him immediately.

What you see is what you get, said Merrick. I used to think there must be a skeleton in his closet but I've known him five years now, been on residentials with him and everything and I can't find one if there is. I've never met a boss like him. He seems to care about everyone who works for him.

I guess some people are just the real deal, I said.

Maybe, Merrick said.

He sat back in his seat and we were silent in the dark of the car until he spoke again.

I'll tell you something about David though, but you're never to mention it. Do you hear me?

Of course, I won't say a thing.

You've got to promise me. It's between us.

I promise.

He used to be married.

Yes, I noticed the wedding ring.

His wife was murdered.

Really? God, that's horrible. What happened?

You can find it in the papers. Google it. It's all there. It was a big story. She was kidnapped. Missing for weeks. When the cops eventually tracked her down she was dead. The murderer had her locked in his bathroom. She was tied up. He'd kept her there as his plaything. Then he'd slit her throat.

Fuck, that's horrendous. What happened to the murderer?

He was there when they found the body. They arrested him and he was given a life sentence.

I should think so.

Only he escaped.

He escaped from prison?

Yeah, about a year after he got banged up.

Fuck.

We drove in silence once more. I watched the white eyes in the road.

They never found him then? I said at last.

Nope.

He's still out there?

I suppose so.

I looked out of the window and the night struck a sinister tone.

We sat in silence again. We were close to Merrick's house now. As I pulled up outside his door he unclicked his seat belt.

Thanks for the lift, he said.

Don't mention it.

He opened the door, then turned to me.

Listen, it's not a secret or anything. Like I say, you can Google it. It's all there. But don't ever mention it. If he finds out you've spoken to anyone about it, he'll fire you. Then he'll fire me.

Don't worry, I said. I don't intend to tell anyone. I promise.

When I got back, Lisa was still up. She was watching television and drinking wine.

Nice night? she asked.

I poured myself a glass, sat down on the sofa beside her, and despite what I had just promised my line manager, I told her about David.

That's some story, she said.

I know, I know. It's horrific.

She picked up the iPad.

What are you doing? I said.

Googling it.

We read the newspaper reports. It was all there, just as Merrick had said. There was a picture of the murderer. He was in his thirties. Fair haired. A prominent gap between his two front teeth, but apart from that there was nothing remarkable about him. There was a picture of David's wife too. She was called Isabella. In the picture she looked like she was in her early forties. She was petite, with a dark complexion. She had big round eyes and long dark wavy hair. She was wearing a white dress. She looked beautiful.

How awful, I said.

We stared at her image for a while.

Why does it always feel more tragic when the victim is attractive? Lisa said.

It was an odd thing to say, but I knew what she meant.

We talked a bit more. I made Lisa promise me she wouldn't talk to anyone else. Then we went to bed.

Over the next few months I settled into my new role. I was breaking new performance records and smashing sales targets. I was enjoying my success and my growing reputation. One night, David invited Lisa and I over for a meal. Lisa drove, as she had an upset stomach and didn't want to drink. David was the perfect host. He greeted Lisa at the doorway. Kissed her on both cheeks. Lisa warmed to him straight away. He was a good cook too. He served pan-fried sea bass with a white crab salad. His house was capacious but not too lavish. There were no conspicuous displays of wealth but everything inside had been chosen to create an overall effect of comfort and good taste.

As Lisa drove us back, we talked about the murder again for the first time.

He doesn't seem troubled, Lisa said.

How do you mean? I said.

Well, you know, you'd expect something like that to stain your character. You'd expect to take something like that with you wherever you went. Like a shadow. Like a scar.

It was over ten years ago. Maybe you get over it, I said.

No, surely not. How can you get over something like that?

We didn't speak for the rest of the drive. Lisa pulled up in the driveway and we climbed out. When we got to the door, I reached for the keys, but they weren't in my pocket.

Shit, I said.

What's the matter?

I can't find the keys.

You're joking, right?

I rummaged through every pocket. Then I had a thought. As we were getting into the car at David's place I'd tipped up my jacket. They must have fallen out onto the grass.

You fucking idiot, Lisa said.

I know, I'm sorry.

I'll have to drive you back, she said. You've drunk too much.

I know, I said, I'm really sorry.

Lisa parked a little way from David's house. It was late now, and we didn't want to disturb him. I got out and left the door ajar so as not to make a noise. I went to where we had parked on the lawn near the driveway. I didn't have to search for long. The moon was almost full and its silver light was reflected on the metal of the keys. Just as I had thought, they were there in the grass. I picked them up and put them in my pocket. I turned to walk back to the car, but as I did I heard a loud 'thunk' sound. It came from behind David's house.

My first thought was that it was a burglar. I crept round the back and peered behind the hedge. At first I couldn't see anything, but then the moon lit up a brick outbuilding. It looked like it had been a stables perhaps, or a storage barn. Then I saw David opening a metal door in the side of the building. He'd swung open a barred metal grate that covered the door and I assumed this was what had made the noise. He held a bag in one hand and a key in the other. As he opened the door, he was briefly silhouetted in a rectangle of white light. Then he went inside. It was past midnight. I decided it was none of my business and I got back into the car.

What were you doing back there? Lisa said as she drove off.

I thought I heard a noise, I said.

And?

It was nothing.

I don't know why I didn't tell her.

Two weeks went by and still I didn't tell Lisa. One night she was out with some girlfriends. I had the night to myself. I didn't feel like drinking. I thought about watching something on television. I sat down in the armchair and flicked through the channels. I did this several times before switching it off. Something was bothering me. It was the white rectangle of light. Why was it such a bright light? What was David doing? Was he growing something? What had been in the bag? It was really none of my business but I couldn't get it out of my mind. Eventually, I picked up the car keys and drove over to David's.

I killed the lights before I got anywhere near the house and parked a good way from it. I slunk round the back, treading very carefully. I stayed behind the hedge for almost an hour, my hands and ears numb with the cold, before I saw David make his way over to the outbuilding. He was carrying the bag again. I watched him as he put the bag down by the side of the grate. I watched him unlock the grate and swing it open, making the 'thunk' noise again. Then I watched him unlock the door, his silhouette in the rectangle of light once more, before disappearing inside.

A minute or so later David came back out of the building. He wasn't carrying the bag this time. He walked across the courtyard and back into his house. This was my chance. Creeping in the shadows, I made my way across.

In the bleached light, my eyes struggled to adjust. At first the room was bare, but then I saw it. I blinked. I moved closer. He, if indeed it was a *he*, because its genitals had been removed, was standing in a barred cage, approximately two foot square, so that the bars were all around it leaving no space to move. Not that it – he – could have moved anyway. One of its arms was fastened by a chain round one of its wrists. The chain was attached by a ring to the ceiling. The length of the chain made it possible for the thing to stand but only on tip-toe. The links of the chain were orange with rust. Its extended arm had long since atrophied and died and was now like a dead branch jutting out of a near-dead tree. Its other arm was free to move, but the only thing it could reach was a tray in front of it, which was filled with a thick gruel that looked like wet cement. On the floor beside the cage, I could see the bag that David had brought. The rest of the gruel was spilling out of the top.

The thing was skin and bone. There was no muscle left whatsoever. The nails on the withered hand of the thing were like snail shells and it took great effort for it to scoop up the gruel and transfer it to its mouth. Half the time it missed and the chest and abdomen of the thing were caked in the dried remnants of the gruel.

It was in perpetual light. There was a spotlight in the corner of the room which I assumed glared at the thing day and night. The temperature of the room was hot enough to sustain life but not warm enough to provide comfort.

The thing was naked. It had hair growing in patches. Some of the hair on its head reached down to the base of its spine, but there were bald spots. Its lips had long since been reduced to two cracked lines.

Its eyes were hardly open. And it groped for the gruel without really looking. It was standing in its own shit and piss, which was also caked along its legs. The stench was overpowering, making me gag, but it was clear that it must get washed away from time to time for it was less than an inch thick. Its skin was scabbed and red in places, covered in weeping sores. The smell of the septic puss mingled with the stench of effluence. As I stared at the thing, I felt a curious mix of repulsion, horror and pity. Then the thing lifted its head, opened its eyes some more and stared directly at me. I felt ice water rush through my veins. It opened its mouth wider and tried to speak. As the lips parted I could see clearly the gap between the two front teeth. But nothing came out, other than a faint croak. I fought the impulse to run away.

I stared for some time. I imagined that it whispered, 'kill me'. Because the kindest thing to do would be to snap its frail neck, but there was no way to get access to the cage. A heavy padlock guarded the door. I thought about coming back with a knife, or even a stick, to put it out of its misery. I heard a sound outside – David. I quickly slunk out and hid behind the hedge again.

I saw David return. This time with a bucket. I presumed it was full of water and he was going to use it to wash away the stinking effluence.

I turned away and walked to my car. As I drove to my house, I was determined to return. What the thing had done was repellent, and it deserved to be punished, but what I had witnessed was something that no creature should have to endure. Ever. That night I had nightmares. In my nightmares the thing was there. I was the thing. Then we swapped and the thing was chasing me. When I woke I told myself not to be stupid. I could never be the thing. And the thing could never come after me. In the morning Lisa asked if I was okay? I had woken her several times with my screams. I assured her it was just a silly dream. I didn't tell her about the thing.

For two or three nights I slept like this and during the day it was no better. The thing was constantly on my mind. One night, when Lisa was asleep, I drove back over to David's place. I found a window at the back of the shed and forced it open. I crawled inside. I watched the thing, quite still, in the bright light. I couldn't tell if it was awake or not. I'd come to rescue it, but now, staring at the deformed, emaciated body, smelling its repulsive odour, I was less sure about my actions. Then I thought about Isabella. I saw her dark wavy hair. She was wearing the white dress. I don't know why I did it, but I picked up some garden shears that were hanging from a hook on the wall. I walked over to the thing and poked it with the shears in its side, piercing its flesh. It cried out. I dropped the shears, climbed back through the window, and ran off. Later that night I lay down beside Lisa. I closed my eyes and pushed the image of the thing out of my mind.

A year has now passed. The board are talking about making me chief marketing officer. We've moved to a bigger place with a huge garden. In one corner is a hot tub. Just as I predicted, Lisa used it three times when it was first installed but never since. Sometimes, when she is out with her friends, I take a walk round the garden and stand close to its girth. I watch the still circle of water, clouds mirrored on its surface, flies dancing above the film. They seem to be attracted to its coolness. To its blackness. Sometimes when I look into it, I imagine that it goes on forever. The black vat of water has no end. But one time when I stared into the blackness I saw the atrophied eye of the thing staring back.

just a job

I'd been working that patch for about ten months when he drove up. He gave me the money, straight away, said that were just for accepting his offer. I counted it, more than I'd make all night. He said he didn't want to know my name. I asked him where he wanted to drive to, they don't always know, and I've got a few quiet spots I use. He said he would take me to a hotel. It'd never happened like that before. One time I went back to this bloke's house. His wife was there. It was weird. He wanted to watch while me and her fingered each other. But a hotel. That were a new one. I had a flick knife in my bag. The stuff helped. I'd only just shot it up. My head was still fucked.

When we got to the hotel the receptionist asked for a credit card. I'll pay cash, he said, and took out his wallet. But the woman, I think she were Polish or Russian or something, said they needed a card as well. This is rule, she said. So he took out his wallet and handed her another roll of notes. He asked for a room service menu and ordered wine from it. We took the lift to the sixth floor. He were talking about something but I weren't paying attention.

The room was at the end of the corridor. There was a king-size bed and a lounge area. He took off his jacket and hung it in the wardrobe. He sat down on a sofa and switched on the telly opposite. He flicked through the stations. Make yourself comfortable, he said. Sit here. He patted the sofa. We watched *Game of Thrones*. There were a knock on the door. The porter with the wine and two glasses. He tipped him and closed the door. He sat back down, opened the wine, and poured us both a glass. He wanted to talk to me about what the other men did. Said he got off on it. What do they like? The usual. Had I come across anything a bit out of the ordinary? I don't do anal, I said. I didn't mean that. Then, what? I don't do gang bangs if that's what you mean. I just want to know, how easily shocked you are. I told him that I'd been around. He nodded. He seemed satisfied with this. But he still quizzed me for ages, until I said, look, are we going to do this or not? Very well, he said. Then he started kissing me. I told him there were no kissing, but he took his wallet out again and handed me another roll of notes, more than last time. I put it in my bag next to the knife.

He had those eyes that sink into the back of the head so that they're always in shadow. It were a right posh pad. There were paintings on the walls and fresh flowers in a vase. He took out some masking tape, a pair of rubber gloves, and a scalpel. He told me to undress. I thought about running but the door were too far away. My bag was by my side. The flick knife. I went for it, but he stopped me. Slapped me. Pushed the bag under the sofa. Take your clothes off, he said. I won't ask you again. Do it slowly. On the telly there were this dwarf in a weird leather tunic thing.

I was cut quite bad afterwards. I didn't work for two weeks. I made enough money from that one job to take some time off. You don't expect them to like you. You don't want them to. It's just. I mean. He needed to see blood. That's how he got off.

I didn't think I'd see him again. The way he left, it were a bit final. I didn't want to see him again. I mean, I've been smacked. I've had my head kicked in. I got it so bad one time I were in intensive care. I kept telling myself I was going to get off the stuff. Every time I scored, I told myself it were the last bag. But it was my lad. The thought of him. I'd be fine. I'd be doing ok. Then I'd be in a shop or a café, and I'd see a young mum with her child, and it would just overtake me. I couldn't breathe. Couldn't get air in my lungs. It's like. Being buried. Alive. It was too much. I just couldn't take the pain.

I were in a trap. I needed the stuff to block out the pain of not seeing him, but I couldn't see him while I was on the stuff. That's what they said. I tried to keep my head down. Just work, sleep, shooting up. At the end of the day, it's just a job. I hate it. Course I do. But I'd hate cleaning toilets for a living or wiping old folks' arses. I kept saying to myself, if I can just get enough, to get away, start somewhere else. You need to break the cycle. That's what they told me. But it was just a dream. A fantasy.

Then, one night, on the same street, this dark car with a really quiet engine pulls up. It's him. I say no at first. I don't want to. He offers me more money. Double what he'd paid last time. I still said no, it want worth it. So he doubles it again. It was some months after and all the cuts had healed. It's not like getting punched or kicked. The cuts heal really quick. And I thought, with that money, you know, I could quit the job, move somewhere else. Get off the stuff and get some different work. I thought about getting a burger van. Maybe they'd let me see him if they saw that I were coping.

So I open the door and I get in. He nods and drives off. Not so much as a smile. You don't expect them to like you. You don't want them to. Not really. It's just work, I tell myself, as we drive down the street. It's just a job. That's how you have to think about it.

baby snakes

I handed him a bottle of cheap red and he said, Come in. He smiled as he put it in the fridge. I know nothing about red wine but I know it's served at room temperature. The house was small and crammed with piles of clothes, bedding and boxes. There was an Indian dream catcher trinket hanging from the corner of the ceiling covered in cobwebs.

We were in the kitchen. The house had an open staircase which went through the middle of the room. There was just a thin rail on one side and nothing on the other. They had made use of this – each step was a shelf with pans and kitchen utensils on. She was coming through from the other room with place mats and condiments. Her long red hair loosely tied – stray strands playing across her face. She looked like Elizabeth Siddal. She saw me and ran over – excited. She greeted me with, Hello. I think her excitement was nerves. She clung to the salt and pepper shaker.

This is Ned. Ned, this is Nick, she said.

We've already met, I said.

We exchanged glances.

There's plenty to eat, it's nothing special – are you hungry?

Was I hungry? I had to think, you get used to it. She ushered me into the living room. It was cosy with clutter. Two sofas at right angles. A square table. There was a TV and a piano and stool in one corner. The walls were lined with shelves – books and records. Hundreds of them.

Make yourself at home, would you like a drink?

I was thinking quick. A glass of red, ta. I had to rescue it. She disappeared again. The books were an odd mix. Mostly hippie literature – Herman Hesse, Carlos Castenada, Timothy Leary. There was a small collection of Crowley lurking between books on nutrition and stuff on the English Civil War. There were books on Native Americans and a great big fat tome on the I-Ching. The records were also an eclectic mix. Lots of prog rock, 60s psychedelia, plus Stockhausen, Sun Ra and Herbie Hancock. There was a slim section of folk, Joni Mitchell, Crosby Stills and Nash, stuff like that. Then, standing on their own shelf, nearly a hundred Frank Zappa albums. This intrigued me, the sheer extent of it, in chronological order it seemed. I'd never heard any Zappa. I wanted to know what it sounded like. I made my mind up to start there, see how far I could get.

The tea was ready and I was ushered to the kitchen table. Ned was dishing out the food. There was couscous, raita, tabbouleh, falafel, various salad things, boiled potatoes. Each item in itself looked interesting. But piled up on a plate they began to resemble the chaos of their surroundings. He passed this across to me and started on another unsuspecting plate. Pam pulled up a chair, her hair freeing itself from a loose felt wrap.

So have you made up your mind then? Ned asked.

Eh?

About looking after the house?

Oh yeah, I laughed, No problem, what's it for, a week?

There were piles of brown boxes in heaps. Ned had his own organic veg business. Home delivery.

Eight days. We wouldn't ask, only Samain has just had kittens and we think it's best if someone is there for her.

I nodded. I love cats, I lied. He nodded back.

I'd been here before, when Ned had been out on his deliveries. He was twisting a plait of hair, which dangled down his spine like the coyote tail on a Davy Crockett hat. I guessed his hair had been long once and this singular strand was a souvenir. I wondered if he knew I was screwing his girlfriend. I'm sure he did. I could tell by the way he was sizing me up, pretending to be friendly so he could get the measure of me. They had an open relationship. At least he did. As far as I could tell this was the first time she'd tested that side of things. I really did try and make an attempt to eat the food. I made an excuse.

I didn't realise we were having a proper meal, I've already eaten.

Pam came to my rescue. You eat what you can, it will all keep in the fridge.

There was a boy, about fourteen, skulking in a darkened area of the room. I think he was playing with a games console. He kept his head down. Pam had two kids, a daughter and a son. I presumed this was her son though we weren't formally introduced. I had already met her nine-year-old daughter, Zee. The son was from a former relationship, you could sense something between him and Ned, sly furtive glances. Hateful eyes. I offered to wash up, but Ned butted in.

No, it's OK, that's his job.

He stared at the boy. The boy didn't budge. We went through to the living room. I began building up a spliff, but Ned produced some sort of ethnic pipe device and started cooking up some black.

We don't smoke it with tobacco. Tobacco is a poison.

I put my things back in the pouch and buried them in the lining of my jacket. We talked about the job. The job of looking after the house. They were going on holiday, taking the kids with them. They couldn't pay me but I could have as much organic veg as I could eat and there was beer in the garage if I got thirsty. He'd leave his block of hash behind for me to finish. It was a big block. And the bed. They had a waterbed and he said that I could sleep on it. All I had to do was keep an eye on the cat. She'd be no trouble. He'd leave me the number of his mobile. It sounded fine to me. I was between jobs. I planned to use the time to get my head together. Sort my life out. In the evening there were women I could invite. The waterbed. I would also get to know Frank.

Where's the cat?

I hadn't seen it yet.

She's in the airing cupboard in the bathroom, with her kittens, she'll probably stay there most of the time. Just put food out for her regular, that's the main thing.

And Zee?

She's staying over at a friends.

Pam came into the room with beer cans and some glasses. Her son was lagging behind. Ned told him to put on a CD. I was surprised with all the vinyl around that he wanted to play a CD. I joked – Were the records just for special occasions? He just shrugged and asked me what I fancied. I didn't know, though I admitted to an interest in Zappa.

I don't know his stuff. Where's a good place to start?

Ned suggested Joe's Garage. The boy took the disc out of its case and put it in the machine. The music started to play. A rock beat with a sinister whisper over the top. Then some comic sound effects. Pam seemed a little more relaxed now, she even managed a secret smile, while Ned was distracted with his pipe. I'd only been seeing her for a few weeks, but already it was getting intense. I think she was a bit out of practice. She spent most of her day with Zee, as she had withdrawn her from school a few years ago. She did tell me, but I can't remember the reason. So it was her job to provide an education. She also told me that she was still breastfeeding her. I was shocked, but she said, it was perfectly normal. It was only a capitalist patriarchy that found it subversive.

She was talking about Steiner, then Jung. Then she was talking about cancer. Apparently she'd had a tumour a few years ago and had got rid of it with a special diet. Most of this consisted of carrot juice. She was reaching for a book, removing the one about this cure. Her legs were open wide. Her cropped top rising up to her bra as she reached across. I was thinking about last night. I had fucked her from behind while Ned was at a mate's.

I don't know how long we sat there in a stoned haze. We drifted into conversations. Drifted back out again. The music was beginning to grate. I looked over at Pam's son, still with his head down. He shot me a look. He smiled to himself. It occurred to me that we had been listening to the same track, for possibly as long as an hour. Either that, or Frank was a washout.

Are all these songs supposed to sound the same?

Ned came out of his trance for a moment. He listened. Realisation creased his forehead. He looked over at the machine then at Pam's son.

What've you done..? You've put the first track on repeat, you little twat.

Pam's son stood up, laughing to himself. He left the room. Ned walked over to the machine and took off the repeat function. He forwarded it to the next track. For some reason I can't explain I was really annoyed about what had happened, even though I'd only just noticed. It was a joke aimed at Ned but we all suffered. Pam's son had the mind of a terrorist.

Time ran round in circles. Subjects were touched on – circumnavigated. Pam was on about reincarnation.

Oh yeah, Ned believes he's been around for thousands of years, whereas I'm relatively new to it. This could even be my first incarnation.

Funny how there's always a hierarchy. Pam seemed a little bitter about it, understandably – though not angry at Ned. I figured if there was reincarnation I'd like to come back as a giraffe so that my head would be clear of all this smoke. The room was filling up with it. My eyes were sore and my throat dry, but I was too stoned to do anything about it.

I had stopped contributing to the conversation a while ago and was now sat back watching it all from a distance. Not that there was much to watch. I got up and thanked them for the meal. I shook hands with Ned. He had stopped scrutinising me now.

Nice meeting you. He nodded lazily.

Pam was getting up.

I'll see myself out.

She seemed relieved. As I walked back into the kitchen towards the front door, I noticed a fried egg on the wall. I was curious, but not enough to go back and ask them.

I went round first thing, helped Ned load the roof rack, saw them off with a wave. Zee seemed excited, but the boy was sat over his games console again, chin in chest. I hadn't brought much with me, just a small holdall of clothes. I took it upstairs into the bedroom. The bed was huge, much bigger than I had imagined. I presumed they had changed the sheets, they felt clean. I put the bag down and collapsed into the bed.

Waves, my body being rocked. First jostled in different directions. Then, as it calmed down, gentle ripples. I had a sense of the weight beneath me. I could feel my muscles relaxing. I was supported uniformly, like I was lying in a mould of myself. I lay there for some time, my eyes closed. But I couldn't suppress an urge to empty my bladder, must be all the water underneath me.

I got up, wrestled with the rubber mattress as it tried to contain me. As I was taking a leak I remembered what Ned had said about the airing cupboard. I looked over to it, the door slightly ajar. I walked across quietly and opened it. There on the towels was the cat, surrounded by her kittens, I don't know how many, it was hard to count the jumble of chubby little bodies. She eyed me suspiciously. There was something fearless in that look. I shut her back in the warmth and dark again.

I surveyed the house. It was a two bedroomed terrace, with a converted attic, so it didn't take long. I helped myself to a lager from the fridge. It was only ten o'clock in the morning, but there was no reason why I shouldn't. It was my wages.

I carried it into the living room and took out the first Zappa record. Ned had left the block of draw on the table with a note: smoke me. So I did. This time, my way, in a spliff with lots of tobacco. I had to pace myself. By the third Zappa album I was feeling really disconnected. I lay on the carpet looking up at the light fitting. As I stared, the ceiling became the floor. I was the one above, glued to the roof looking down at a bulb on a stalk. The music and the words separated. The music sinking down into a swamp of noise. The words floating above like tossed up flotsam: *baby aby bestkindofpet liveinahole byacode pink I'llgivemadrink baby aby snay.*

By mid-afternoon I decided on an action plan which was simply to go for a walk. The house was beginning to get to me. I was not alone. I don't know why, but the thought of the cat in the cupboard disturbed me.

The air was crisp. My steps sluggish. I walked the pavements. First lots of space, just the hum of traffic, then I was mobbed by children as they spilled out of school for the day. I passed a cordoned off area where a house was being demolished. The front of the house had already gone and the rooms were visible. One of the upstairs rooms had been wallpapered with Thomas the Tank Engine wallpaper. A boy had lived there. He had gone to sleep in that room every night, his head filled with the day's memories, and each morning he had woken, each morning still new and exciting.

When I got back I felt low. I didn't think I would make the week. Time was a starched sheet stretching out in front of me – beneath which it was as unstable as water. The stillness of the house, the cacophony of Zappa records. I dished out a tin of cat food and took out another beer can from the fridge. Time to make phone calls. I rang up two girl friends, invited them for tea. They said yes, they'd be there at six. This is what I needed, a purpose. There was no shortage of food.

After we'd eaten, I told them about the bed. They seemed curious so I took them upstairs. They found it funny, not erotic. They took turns on it. I wasn't invited. They didn't stay late, they were both working. I was alone once more.

When I climbed into the bed that night I felt uneasy, as though I were being watched. The door of the bedroom was open. The bathroom also. In the half darkness of the room I could see two luminous animal eyes, staring into mine.

I dreamt, predictably, that I was at sea. Only it was a different time and I was not a man. I was a woman. In the dream I fucked a sailor. It sounds a bit daft, but at the time it was beautiful. I remember every sensation. His rough kiss, his smooth neck, his hard arms holding my back. The soft hair covering the cleft at the top of his legs. His callused hands.

The next morning the cat food was gone – someone had been feasting while I had been asleep. My new life in the house had already taken on a routine. Beer for breakfast. A walk. Binge on organic veg, select next Zappa album. Skin up. Smoke. Lie back. My evenings were taken up, first with the telephone, attempting to persuade someone to come and join me, secondly with cooking a meal, and last and hardest of all – accepting that no one was coming.

After four days I was feeling strange. How could anyone live like this? I started to read some of the books, and I looked in desperation for a television. There wasn't one. I had started work Monday morning. It was now Thursday – not even four full days. I began searching the house for something to do. I tried the drawers beneath the shelves in the living room. Cassette tapes, thousands of them. They were all filed in alphabetical order. I went through the cupboard, you wouldn't believe the junk people keep: a lead for a kettle, piles of menus for take-away outlets, a shoe horn, some elephant tape, a box of odd socks. There were little tins with things in them: buttons, zips, paper clips, thimbles, travel scrabble.

I found a bigger box, with photographs in it. I started to flick through. Holiday snaps. Kiddies' birthday parties. Then I came across some odd ones of Zee. In one of the photographs she was naked. She was on top of the piano stool, curled up like a foetus. She was looking directly at the camera – confrontational. In another she was stood up. She had on her mother's slip and was holding it up to reveal her genitals. Again she was staring at the camera, or at the person holding the camera. I couldn't make my mind up this time, either she was shy, or scared and trying hard not to show it. I felt a snake crawl up my spine.

I was thinking about the fact that Pam still breast-fed Zee. I had found this out one time when we'd been together and Zee had grabbed hold of Pam's top. Pam had gone red and told her to wait. I hadn't said anything then, but later when we were on our own I had asked her about it. She told me she was still suckling her.

But she's nine years old, isn't she supposed to have grown out of that? I could sense Pam's discomfort and I hadn't pushed it. It seemed even odder now, after seeing the photographs. I put them back in the box.

They were due back the following Monday. I opened two tins for the cat, freshened the water bowl, zipped up my holdall, pocketed the block of draw and left. I posted the key back through the door. Pam rang me Monday evening, but I didn't answer. I didn't answer any of her calls.

I go past there every day now. I've got a new job and the bus goes that way. I always look but never see anyone coming in or out. But the other day, as it drove down their street, an old woman standing at the bus stop put her hand out and the driver braked. I looked over to their house and saw a police car parked outside. Then I saw Ned. Two male police officers were escorting him down the path. His hands were cuffed at the front and his head was bent low. As they approached the vehicle, one officer opened the passenger-side back door. The bus was moving away, but as it did I just saw the back of his head as he climbed in. The neat thin plait of hair dangling down his back – like a rat's tail. The bus drove down the road and turned left. It stopped again outside where I'd seen the half-demolished house. There's another one there now, in its place – exactly the same type. A new family living there. I saw them unloading their car. A man and a woman. Two children – a boy and a girl. For some reason I thought about that Zappa song, Baby Snakes. And I couldn't get the jingle out of my head.

a four letter word

He was flicking through the jobs section of the local paper as he did every day – usual menial positions, or stuff he wasn't qualified or experienced enough to try – when he saw the ad: want to earn £500 a week? Company car. No qualifications or experience necessary, full training will be provided. Ring... He took off the top of his red pen and drew a circle round it. He knew it for what it was – a sales job – but it sounded better than the others, and even if he only earned half of that it was still shitloads more than what the dole paid out.

It seemed to him like he'd been on the dole forever. It hadn't bothered him at first. It was nice to have a bit of free time. He slept in. He watched daytime TV. He went for walks in the park. But gradually, as the days turned to weeks and the months went by, spring became summer and then autumn, the leaves fell from the trees, the nights drew in, there was a chill in the air and it started to get to him. He began to think that work was something that would never happen again. He would go to sign on and look at the rest of the claimants, dressed in cheap sportswear, unshaven. Not unclean exactly, but unkempt. There was a general air of shabbiness. What was the point in making an effort? Who would want to employ this lot? Then he would think, but you are one of them. Why would anyone want to employ you?

The image of a job was fading in his mind, so that it was merely a sketch of an idea. A thin outline.

He saw it from the other side: the longer he signed on the less employable he became. From the point of view of the man in the suit sitting behind his desk. Why would he employ someone who had spent so long in enforced idleness? You lose your confidence. You lose your skills. You become less sociable. The dole killed some people. His mates had cracked up. One an agoraphobic, another a crook. His former best mate had taken to quoting long passages of the Old Testament to his Jack Russell. Another had been found in the bath. An overdose. It wasn't just the lack of money, but that was tough. He lived on black tea and jam sandwiches. Once a fortnight he'd have a few pints in the pub but he couldn't enjoy it. A mate who was working would buy him a pint out of generosity, but it would nag at him. He would feel indebted to him. He would feel beneath him and he felt pretty low as it was. He didn't want to feel indebted to his friend. He didn't want to feel beneath him. Occasionally he managed to supplement his dole with a bit of casual labour: cleaning out some gutters, painting and decorating, a bit of gardening. But then the work would dry up and he'd go back to his flat and his empty fridge.

He would stare at the walls. He would lie on the floor and look up at the ceiling, at the magnolia paint congealing on the plaster rose around the light fitting. He would go to the window and watch the cars drive past: going to work, coming from work. He would watch people stand at the bus stop and queue for a bus: going to work, coming from work. He would watch the people on the bus playing with their phones or reading a paper: going to work, coming from work. He felt outside of society. The world was out there. Things were happening. People were living. But he was stuck in his flat. His life had stopped. He had nothing. He could feel the cold accrete about him. He was twenty-three.

He looked at the ad again. He stared at the words until they blurred and danced in front of his eyes. Then he took out his phone and punched in the number. Hello, my name is Andrew Green, I'm calling about the ad in the paper. The receptionist asked him some questions. He answered them the best he could even though he felt foolish doing so. He was a loser, surely she could hear it in his voice. He was surprised at the end of the call when he was invited in for an interview. Could he make such and such a date? He said he'd have a look in his diary. He didn't have a diary. There was no point as he didn't have anything to put in it. After a long pause, he picked up the phone again. Yes, he could make that date. He said he looked forward to meeting her and terminated the call.

The next day he decided to walk into town to buy a new shirt. He had a suit that was still fairly decent but only one white shirt and it had turned a sort of yellow-grey colour. He had no money and thought about how he could acquire some. He looked around his flat. Surely there was something he could sell. But everything of value had already been exchanged. Then he looked down at his phone. He'd run out of credit on it and he couldn't afford to buy any more. What was the sense in keeping it? He went to a cash converters and used the money they gave him to buy a new white shirt.

At the interview he was asked to complete a test. It wasn't difficult but still, he was shocked by how nervous he was as he wrote his answers down. When it came to the interview his legs felt weak, his throat was dry and the palms of his hands were wet with sweat. There were two men, and they introduced themselves: Chris Obassi, the sales manager, and Trevor Barker, the company director. They both wore pristine white shirts with gold cufflinks, silk ties, gold watches and designer suits. Chris Obassi, was a large black man with a bald head and a thick neck. Trevor was white but with a sun-bed tan that made his skin look orange. He had dark hair that was combed back. It was hard to say how old they were. Chris looked to be younger than Trevor. He guessed they could be anywhere between thirty-five and fifty-five.

When they went to shake his hand, he had to wipe it on his trouser leg first. They asked him to sit down and took their seats behind a massive desk. They asked him about his previous work experience. He gave them a potted history. There wasn't much to tell. Some factory work, some office work.

So, Andy, tell me, what are you afraid of?

He was afraid of so many things. He was afraid of the police. Because they can take you away. They can lock you up. When he was a kid he had a fear of answering the phone. The fear of a really scary voice on the other end. He'd had a black and white TV in his bedroom when he was young. He remembered staying up to watch a film. And there was a phone. A really old-fashioned phone and it just kept ringing and ringing. And he lay in bed and waited for someone to answer the phone. But nobody did.

Oh, you know, the usual things. Nothing much.

Such as?

Well, nothing serious.

Not afraid of the dark?

Well, a bit, I suppose. I mean, I prefer the light.

He laughed but neither man cracked a smile.

What about heights. Are you scared of heights?

He had never been afraid of heights until recently. He'd been paid by a neighbour to clean out his gutters. He'd borrowed a ladder and used some rope to lash the top of the ladder to the gutter. Only, halfway through the job, holding a bucket in one hand and a trowel in the other, the gutter had come away from the wall and the ladder had fallen. He'd managed to jump off safely, with nothing more serious than a twisted ankle, but it had knocked him and when he'd tried to go back up to finish the job he'd got dizzy and anxious. He told the neighbour that he wasn't feeling well and he'd never gone back to complete the work.

A bit, I suppose.

What about nightmares. Do you have nightmares?

He had nightmares constantly. He dreamed about killing people or being killed. He'd wake up sweating. That morning he had dreamed that he was urinating in a public toilet. He was standing over a trough, next to a cubicle and when he looked round, he noticed that the cubicle door was ajar. He could see a man sitting on the toilet with his trousers round his ankles. The man had a big hipster beard. Andy noticed the man had tattoos up his leg. For some reason, Andy had turned to the man and pissed all over him. He had woken up needing the toilet.

No. Not that I remember.

Up to this point, the questions had been asked by Chris Obassi. But now Chris sat back in his chair and gave the nod to Trevor. Trevor pulled his chair closer.

Andy, would you describe yourself as an aggressive person?

He thought hard about this before answering, I wouldn't use that term myself. I prefer the term, assertive.

Trevor looked at Chris and they both pulled disapproving faces. Trevor persisted: Yes, but would you describe yourself as aggressive?

Andy thought it might be a test, that they were seeing if he could stay composed under pressure. He returned the same answer. They carried on asking him the question. Different variations. Over and over. They were winning – he was getting aggressive.

At last he snapped, Yeah, I am aggressive, right!

He was shouting now, his face was red and he brought his fist down hard on the table. That's it, he'd blown it. Or so he thought. The two men smiled at each other. Then Trevor stood up and proffered his Rolex-clad hand. Andy stood up in shock, reciprocating. They shook.

Congratulations, Andy, you've got the job.

Oh, really. That's great. Was it? When do I start?

Training course, Monday morning, nine o'clock.

There were ten of them in total, men in their twenties and early thirties, wearing ill-fitting catalogue suits. Hungry looking. The first morning was company background. Induction stuff. They all went to the pub at lunch. He quickly decided he didn't like his new colleagues. They were so eager – already buying into the company propaganda. Oh, weren't Stoneway great... So much easier to sell when you've got a premium product. They were to sell resin-bonded driveways. No cold calling. Some of them had worked in sales before. Selling double-glazing or fitted kitchens.

This is how it worked: the company would place a full-page glossy advert in a Sunday newspaper colour supplement. A 'before and after' of a house. The 'before' was a horrible drab, concrete path. Cracks and damp patches. Weeds growing out of the cracks. The 'after' was glowing with colour and uniformity. A neat sweep of multi-coloured gravel all held together with the resin to create the perfect gravel driveway – one that didn't need any maintenance. A lifetime guarantee. A driveway that would never need replacing. There was no price mentioned in the advert, but there was a free number. When Mrs Jones would ring to inquire, there would be a voice on the other end saying, What a coincidence, Mrs Jones, it just so happens that a surveyor is in your area next week finalising our show drive allocations. Why don't I get him to pop in as he's passing? See what you think? They mostly fell for it. Why not?

They spent days going through the script. They would practice on each other taking it in turns to be Mrs Jones. Once they had memorised every scenario they were deemed ready to go on the road. They were led out to the car park and each member of the team was allocated a company car: black Fiat Tempras, two litre, electric everything. Nice tidy motors. Andy's first assignment was somewhere in Kent. He was based in Manchester. He calculated that it would take him the best part of five hours to get there, down the M6 to Birmingham, then along the M1, M25, M2, A299 and finally the A28. Just passing?

Andy took the key from Chris Obassi and climbed into the car. He felt successful inside the plush interior as soon as he sat behind the wheel. Chris waved him off. Andy drove out of the centre of Manchester and bombed it down the M6 to Birmingham. A speed camera flashed but it didn't slow him down. He was psyched up after his week of training, ready to take on the Mr and Mrs Jones of the world.

He got to Margate in good time. The satnav had only underestimated the time of arrival by about half an hour. He stopped for a coffee before parking up outside the customer's house: Mr and Mrs Barnett.

He knocked on the door and explained that he was a surveyor, in the area for the day. They were expecting him and invited him in. They were a middle-aged couple whose children had fled the nest. He sat on their sofa and nursed a mug of tea, going through the script with them. They were sitting opposite, in matching armchairs.

Well, Mrs Barnett, I'm glad you asked. Resin is the strongest substance known to man. They inject it into concrete apartments in areas of notorious earthquakes. Nothing. You can crank it up to ten on the Richter scale and that stuff holds up. It's a miracle, you're getting the very best in resin-bonded driveway technology.

You don't see it over here much.

No, you don't. That's because it's new. The Yanks have gone for it big time. They don't mess about do they? They know when they're on to a good thing. We're always a bit behind in this country, always a bit reticent. But imagine it, Mrs Barnett. Imagine it if you can, you'll be the envy of all your friends, pretty soon they'll all want one. But you'll know you were first.

You'll know they all copied off you.

Somewhere in a corner of the room was another Andy watching this Andy going through the script. The Andy that watched did so with great embarrassment. In the offices of Stoneway, the script had seemed a lot more convincing. Now it sounded hollow. He could hear his own voice, it sounded like escaping gas. Chris Obassi had trained the team. He assured them it would work. Stick to the script, was his mantra. He said that if you stuck to the script you would make the sale. But Andy could see already that he was losing Mr and Mrs Barnett. Mr Barnett had already gone back to his TV programme and Mrs Barnett's smile was starting to take on the shape of a grimace.

He struggled on for another ten minutes. Then Mr Barnett turned on him.

If you're a surveyor, where's your camera?

Andy could feel the heat travel through his cheeks and knew that they must be bright red. He tried to come up with an answer. He stammered something. He could feel himself deflating in front of them. He staggered on for another minute or two, until Mr Barnett showed him to the door.

The next day back at base, he waited with his peers for the bollocking off Chris. None of them had made a sale. Chris led them all into a conference room. He told them to sit at the table. He started off by asking them how long they had lasted and then explained where they'd gone wrong. They had to believe in themselves, they had to stoke the fire in their bellies. It was personal. Were they going to let some snotty little civvy keep them from their justly earned money?

Chris pulled up his sleeve, This is a Rolex watch. Do you know how much that cost? These shoes are handmade, Italian. That car parked outside is a Ferrari 599 GTB Fiorani F1. Every night I eat out at the best restaurants in town. Look at you lot, in your Burton suits and your shoes from fuck knows where? Is that what you want to be? A bunch of sad twats in cheap clobber?

He looked around the room.

Well, carry on then. You're going about it the right way.

Then he turned to Andy, What's your story?

Andy told him how it had played out. Chris gave him what for, shouting like an evangelical preacher, pacing the room for effect, before lowering his voice.

Listen, Andy, don't let it get to you. But you have got to anticipate more. You should have said your camera was in the car. You've got to think on your feet. When you lie, do it with a smile.

When Chris told them what to say, they could see how it could work – it was easy. He was totally convincing. And intimidating. His eyes were fiery with the compulsion to sell people something only he knew they absolutely must have. He'd only worked for the company for a few years, and look at him already. One of those posh yuppie apartments on the Quays, top of the range sports car. He wouldn't be seen dead in anything other than Gucci or Armani. He laughed at them in their cheap suits. Is that what they wanted – off the peg crap from Next? Or even worse, H & M? Were they going to be suckers like Mr and Mrs Jones or were they going to be something special? There were winners and losers in life. They had to decide which they wanted to be.

Chris turned to Andy again, Look, kid, you've got a choice. Do you want to be signing on for the rest of your life, with all the dossers and bums, or do you want to be like me, a success, eating out at fine restaurants every night? Drinking champagne, eating foie gras.

The words 'foie gras' had a peculiar effect on Andy. He had read an article about it only recently. It meant 'fat liver'. Andy saw the jaws of a goose forced open with a tube stuck down its throat. He saw hundreds of these geese all being force fed and he felt sick. This must have registered on his face because Chris slapped him on the back.

You don't even know what foie gras is, do you, kid? Not to worry, you'll learn.

Chris laughed. A deep booming laugh.

When Andy left that afternoon he was all fired up again. This time he was not leaving until he'd made a sale. That was the deal. Chris had made it quite clear. They were not to leave the premises until they'd sold. This time he had a Canon camera on a strap around his neck. He'd borrowed it from a friend. The presentation they'd rehearsed lasted about three hours. That included a full description, history, sample blocks. A picture book filled with before and after. A full range of colours, stones, textures. A measuring up of the space to work out a figure. The deal. The finance package – hidden interest on the instalments. And after, and only after every nuance of script had been put across, the closure. As he drove along the motorway, he played it all out in his head like it was a film.

Well Mr and Mrs Jones, I've just finalised the last of the show drives, that's why I'm in your area, and I shouldn't really do this – Chris, my boss, will lynch me in the morning when he finds out – but you've such a nice house, and I'm not being funny, don't take this the wrong way, but the driveway does let it down, doesn't it? To be quite frank with you, Mr and Mrs Jones, your house would make a fantastic before and after.

Now they're interested, they fish for a bit before asking the inevitable. Will it alter the price?

Now, Mrs Jones, it would in fact alter the price considerably. We could knock off 25% from the original quotation, which I'm sure you'll agree will make a substantial difference... Let's see, your driveway we said would cost £3,000, and I know that sounds like a lot, but you're getting the best money can buy, and let's face it, you could get a couple of gypsies to tarmac it for a few hundred quid, but as soon as the frost comes it'll crack up and the next thing it'll look a complete mess. You'll probably get no more than twelve months out of it. You might as well take your couple of hundred and use it to start the fire. Whereas our driveway, as I said before, will last forever, absolutely guaranteed.

He looked at himself in the rear-view mirror. You can do this, Andy, yes you can. But why 'gypsies'? It might offend some people. Surely he could substitute this for 'fly-by-nights' or something else? But Chris had been adamant. Stick to the script. Andy carried on with his rehearsal.

Now, let's tap it into the calculator. The miracle now of converting the overblown price he originally quoted into the actual RRP. And it comes out at £2,250 which I'm sure you'll agree is a superb price for a superior driveway surface of this quality. You can set it and forget it, use it and abuse it. It'll look as good in twenty years as the day it's laid... Now, Mrs Jones, don't snap my hand off. I've not promised you anything. I'm putting my job on the line here you understand, but I can see how much it means to you, so if you want I can ring my boss and beg him to add another to the list. The phone's just through here, is it? Thank you.

Would they wonder about that? What kind of surveyor doesn't have a mobile phone? He would make up some excuse. It had ran out of charge.

That was plausible.

Now, Mr and Mrs Jones, I've rang my boss, he wasn't happy, I got him out of the bath – he's just chewed my ear off. But once he'd calmed down I managed to persuade him. I told him what nice people you were, and of the palatial driveway potential your property has. But what I'll need to do is get a third of the total in cash or cheque tonight before I leave and both your names on the contract... Yes, if you like we can sort out finance, I can do that right now. I realise you're a bit strapped and it'll make it easier.

If he could just get one job where it went anything like that. He was now into the end of his first week on the road, two weeks with the company. He'd had a few near misses but nothing definite. He was yet to make a sale. Each morning it was the same rigmarole – the group humiliation. They would have to go through the entire previous day's scenario in front of their peers, and then the rest would have to proffer their explanation as to where they went wrong: he didn't sell the finance successfully, he didn't list all the advantages a Stoneway driveway has over its competitors. He messed up the show drive closure. This took up most of the morning, but it was shortening. Slowly, his peers were making their virgin sale. A lad called Mohammed had been the first and they'd bought him a watch and a new suit as an example to the eager neophytes, as well as his commission. Then Frank had sold. It was easy for him, he'd come from Safe Windows, selling overpriced PVC frames and doors to zero-hour workers from the council estates, and he'd been thrown out of almost as many doors as he'd actually knocked on.

By the end of day thirteen there were only three of them left in the humiliation room, the rest had done it – the impossible. These three were failures. Each night it had been the same. Go through the script, cover everything, don't leave the house until you'd sold.

He was in a detached house near Aberdeen. It had taken him over six hours to get there. He'd spent two hours going through the script. The couple, a Mr and Mrs Silver, had been very friendly at first, but now they had run out of patience. They made it clear that they wanted him to go. Only Chris had made a new condition for the three that were left without a sale. They would have to ring him before they left the house.

I'm sorry about this, Mrs Silver, but would you mind if I made a quick phone call?

She looked at her husband and he shrugged.

I suppose so. It's in the hall.

Hello, Chris, it's me, I'm in Mr and Mrs Silver's house.

The one on the coast?

That's the one.

Are they saying they want to think it over?

Yeah...

Have you tried the closure? The show drive?

Of course.

And?

Not interested. They want to shop around.

Have they been looking at block paving?

Yeah.

Did you tell them it's just cut up concrete? That they're paying over the odds for plain old ordinary cement, dyed and cut into pretty shapes?

Yeah.

Did you use the example of teeth removal?

Yeah.

Did you tell them you only need to remove one and the rest go loose?

Yeah.

Did you tell them they'd be dicing with death every time they walked out their door?

Yeah.

What about water absorption? Did you tell them the frost will crack them?

Yes. They still want to look around.

Hit them with subsidence.

It won't work.

Try it.

But –

Just...

Sorry about that, Mrs Silver, I just needed to check the facts with my boss. He says we can offer a further reduction, as your property is so suitable.

Chris hadn't mentioned a reduction. In fact, Andy had decided to deduct his commission from the sale. He had to make the sale, even if it meant he would get no money for his trouble.

We've already explained, we want to get a few more quotes first. Now, if you don't mind, I think it's time you went.

I'm sorry, Mrs Silver, do you mind if I make another very quick phone call? I'll give you some money to cover it.

Mr Silver shook his head but Mrs Silver begrudgingly pointed the way to the hall again.

Chris, it's me again. Really, Chris, it's, it's not going to work... I have, I've tried that, I've tried everything... Ok, I'll go and get them...

I'm sorry about this, Mr and Mrs Silver, but would one of you mind coming to the phone? My boss would like a word with you.

Mr Silver stood up and went to the phone, but instead of talking to the voice on the other end, he slammed it down. He took hold of Andy's suitcase and thrust it at him.

I won't tell you again. Get out of this house.

Mr Silver took hold of the samples and thrust them at Andy.

According to Chris there was no such thing as a non-sale, just a non-salesperson. You could always improve, try a different angle, change your attitude. He'd spent three hours with him the next morning, going over where he'd gone wrong. Now Andy was travelling up to Dunfermline on the East coast of Scotland. He was the only one left who had not made a sale. He could do this. This job was going to be the one. It was two o'clock before he set off after the morning's de-briefing. He realised now where he'd gone wrong – he'd seen the error of his ways. He didn't hate the customer enough. The way Chris explained it, it all made sense. The money Mr and Mrs Silver had was actually his money and they had stolen it off him. Was he going to let two gimps like Mr and Mrs Silver steal his hard-earned cash? No, of course not, he was only taking what was rightfully his, even if he had to snatch it off them. It wasn't like he was ripping them off, they were, after all, getting the greatest driveway surface on the planet. They were twisted, misguided sinners, with tiny minds that could only think of concrete and tarmac and flagstones for Christ's sake. It was up to him to show these people the right and true path. Literally.

The appointment had been made for 6 p.m. He had four hours to get there. He got up to the Scottish Borders in reasonable time. He drove towards Edinburgh. It was a sunny day. He had the windows wound down and his sunglasses on. The music was thumping from the two speakers set into the doors. He felt good. He was going to get that money off Mr Kirkpatrick if it was the last thing he did. There was a spliff in the ashtray, 100% sensimillia. It had been sitting there since day eight, when they'd started off on their virgin lead. It was waiting for him to clinch that first deal.

There was 10% commission on each sale. Not bad at all. The average driveway cost was about £4,000. Which meant 400 quid. You only had to make two sales a week and you were loaded. Only with one lead a day it made it sound less feasible. But then there were the extras, the commission on the finance deals, the border stones, the gates and posts. He'd heard of some salesmen making a grand plus on a good week. There were these mythical figures that Chris talked about. A bloke called Joe who'd come out of the army and started with Stoneway. He hadn't even passed the training course but had begged them to let him try again. He'd worked for free till he cracked the script, had it memorised. Then they'd let him out onto civvy street. They called him the Bulldog. Once he bit he just would not let go till he'd clinched it – got the money up front and their moniker in the box. He'd sold to everyone: men, women, rich, poor, black, white, north, south, young, old – no one was immune to his charms or his vice-like grip. Neither Andy nor any of his peers had ever seen 'the Bulldog'. The new team were kept separate from the rest of the sales crew. Annexed into a corner of the office. Partitioned off with plasterboard. They had their own exit and their own entrance.

He reached the Forth Road Bridge on time. He had an hour to find the address. He just had the name and number of the street and a postcode but he felt confident. He listened to the soothing tones of the satnav. Mr and Mrs Kirkpatrick, No.7 Gowanbrae Hill. It sounded prosperous. He followed the instructions on the device and watched the little animated car travel up the map. Then the screen started to flicker. He fiddled with the lead that was plugged into the cigarette lighter socket. The screen stopped flickering. He sat back and relaxed again. He listened to the voice telling him where to go. It was a woman's voice and the manufacturers had obviously chosen her because she could be trusted. She had a voice with that rare combination:

authority and warmth. He needed to cultivate that voice.

He wasn't that far away now. He was feeling good about this one. Surely this sale was his. He looked at the screen again, only it was black. He fiddled with the connection. Nothing. He stopped off at a service station. He switched the device off. Then he switched it back on. Nothing happened. He fiddled with all the connections again and tried to power it up once more. Still nothing. Shit. He could feel the fear grip the back of his throat. Don't panic. You can do this. He got out of his car and went to the cafe inside. He bought a coffee. He bought an A to Z of the area and flicked through the index at the back, found the avenue and marked it up with his pen.

By 7 p.m. he was completely lost. He'd driven round every poxy estate in Dunfermline and still no sign of it. He could see where he had to be on the map, but he just couldn't get to it. He pulled up to a garage.

Gowanbrae Hill?

Never heard of it.

He drove around the streets of Dunfermline, stopping local-looking pedestrians, searching blindly for his Ariadne.

Gowanbrae Hill?

Sorry, mate, not one I know.

Gowanbrae Hill?

Oh, yeah, I think it's up there on the right.

It wasn't up there on the right.

Round and round he went, his heart beating faster, sweat prickling under his cheap synthetic shirt.

Gowanbrae Hill?

Where's it near?

I don't know, it's just Gowanbrae Hill.

What is it your looking for?

Gowanbrae Hill?

And what's there?

Mr and Mrs Kirkpatrick.

No, sorry, pal, can't help you.

It was past eight o'clock when he finally pulled up outside No.7. He allowed himself a breather to get his story straight. Get the camera out. Briefcase. Suit jacket. Adjust tie in rear mirror.

I'm so sorry, really I am. I was held up.

We were told six.

Yes, I know, but something came up I had to sort out.

It's now eight.

I'm here now, won't you let me in? It'll only take a minute.

It was only a small drive. They had a garage but no car. Mr Kirkpatrick had sold it last year. He was eighty-five and had a nervous condition. Mrs Kirkpatrick was explaining all this. She was a bit younger, a bit more on the ball. She seemed annoyed with Andy.

This is a lovely place you have here, Mrs Kirkpatrick. That fireplace, is it slate?

Yes, that's right.

It's very appealing.

Thank you.

I must say, I like your choice of pictures. There's something about water-colours of bowls of fruit that's so life affirming, isn't there?

Oh, I'm glad you like them. We don't know much about art, but we know what we like, don't we, Reg. Would you like a cup of tea? We were just about to have one.

That would be wonderful.

Andy could see her warming to him. And he felt like he'd turned a corner. She went into the kitchen and Andy chatted with Mr Kirkpatrick. She came back into the room balancing three mugs of tea on a rectangular tray. She handed them out.

I must say this tea is delicious. You do make a lovely cup of tea, Mrs Kirkpatrick.

Yes, she said, Reg always says that.

Three hours later they were trying to get him out of the house. They did like the driveway but £3,000 was too much for what they needed. He took his tape measure out.

I could try measuring up again, it does seem a lot but you do get what you pay for.

Mr Kirkpatrick was in his pyjamas, Mrs Kirkpatrick had a nightie on and a woollen house coat. She brought them all a cup of cocoa.

You can drink this and then you really must be off. Reg is normally in bed by ten.

Can I just show you the Stoneway film?

No, really, that's not necessary.

But it shows the Stoneway workmen, how well they prepare the land, how deep they dig the foundations.

It was no use, they were adamant.

Well, if it's a question of money there's a very attractive finance deal I can offer you.

No, absolutely not. We don't believe in borrowing money. You live within your means. We've saved every penny.

He was going to try the lifetime guarantee on them but looking at Mr Kirkpatrick's hands gripping the mug of cocoa he thought better of it. The old man's skin was as thin as a cigarette paper, translucent with big blue veins all along. It was as though the veins were coming to the surface for one last look at the world before drying up entirely.

Then he had a brainwave: Tell me, Mr Kirkpatrick, I hope you don't mind me commenting, but I did notice that you had a stick to assist your walking, and that drive is on a bit of a slope, isn't it. Can I ask you what it's like in winter when Mr Frost has been?

Mr Kirkpatrick's mouth curled up in grin as he explained how he'd nearly gone 'ace over apex' last winter.

I thought so. Hazardous I bet?

Oh aye.

The old man smiled again. It was the most animated Mr Kirkpatrick had been all night.

It's only a matter of time really isn't it before you slip, or worse, Mrs Kirkpatrick slips on it and has a nasty fall.

He let this sink in before continuing.

I don't know if you realise this but all our driveways are 100% non-slip surfaces. Guaranteed.

Really?

Oh yes, didn't I tell you? Well, there you go. The only non-slip driveways you can get.

Mr and Mrs Kirkpatrick gave each other a look.

You know something Mr and Mrs Kirkpatrick, this has been a most pleasant evening. You're such nice people, the cosy room, the tea and biscuits. I'm really very touched by your hospitality. I feel I owe you a favour. Now I did explain when I got here that I'm not a salesman?

They nodded.

I'm a surveyor. I've been up this part of the world all week finalising the last of our show drives.

I see.

We're based in Manchester. You were lucky to catch me like this. Now as I said, I've allocated the last of them, but I'm thinking that you've got such a nice place here, it really would make a superb 'before and after' shot. To be honest, the one I sorted out today was for a Mr and Mrs Jones, and it wasn't nearly as nice as this one. And I'm thinking I could swap theirs for yours. Now Mr and Mrs Jones are not going to be happy about it, but hey, that's life, isn't it?

And would there be a reduction?

That's absolutely correct, Mrs Kirkpatrick, there would in fact be a substantial reduction in cost to you if I were to do that. Now, I'm not promising anything, but if you like I can work it out for you.

If it's no trouble.

No, it's no trouble at all. Now, let's see.

He took out his calculator and tapped in the numbers.

It works out at dead on £2,250, which I'm sure you'll agree is a far more attractive figure.

Well, yes, that is much better.

Now, it really isn't up to me, I'll have to have a word with my boss. He'll probably cut my throat for this.

No harm in trying though?

I'll try my best. Which way's the phone?

Mrs Kirkpatrick showed him where the phone was and offered him another drink.

Oh, thank you, I'd love another cup. OK, wish me luck.

A few minutes later he came back into the room. Mrs Kirkpatrick handed him a mug.

Thanks, that's nice and hot. Now as you heard, it was a pretty heated conversation.

In fact he'd been arguing with Chris's answerphone. Chris switched it on after 11 p.m. as it was not normal for his sales team to ring after that time.

It sounded heated.

Well, I was fighting for you all the way. He's not happy about it, Mr and Mrs Kirkpatrick, but he did finally agree to it. Ha! He'll have me over the coals for this tomorrow, but what the hell, if you can't do two lovely people like you a favour then what's it worth, hey?

Mrs Kirkpatrick helped Mr Kirkpatrick to his feet. He took his walking stick and hobbled over to their bedroom. Andy sat serenely on the sofa smiling at Mrs Kirkpatrick, taking polite sips from his cup. He felt sick. Stress. His heart had been beating double speed all evening but now it had gone into triple time. His stomach was churning up. Behind his back he had his fingers crossed.

Mr Kirkpatrick reappeared with a shoe box under one arm. He managed to make it over to the coffee table where he plonked himself down. The old man removed the lid. The box was stuffed with old wrinkled Scottish five-pound notes.

How much deposit do you need?

I'll need a thousand up front and your monikers just there.

He handed over the paperwork.

Here, use my pen.

He watched them count out the money into twenty piles of ten notes. Each pile being £50. Mr Kirkpatrick counting, Mrs Kirkpatrick tying each one up neatly before returning them to the box.

As he watched them count and arrange the money he relaxed. He gave them the top copy of the contract and folded the rest up and put it into his briefcase. He took the samples, tape measure and DVD back to the boot of his car. It was now past midnight. He was very tired, but he'd done it. He'd actually done it. He'd sold a resin-bonded driveway. The crisp night air tickled his skin. He felt fantastic. The sky was clear of clouds, at first black, but as his eyes adjusted to the dark he saw the stars, the twinkling eyes of fish in a deep lake as they came up for air. Why did they do that when they had gills? He supposed it must feel more real to them. Make them feel like they were truly alive. He took great gulps of the chill night into his chest.

Held it there, watched it smoke as it curled from his mouth. When he went back into the house they had finished counting. Mrs Kirkpatrick sealed up the box with string. He shook both their hands. It really had been very nice meeting them.

It was a long drive back but he didn't care. It was cold, it had been snowing all over the country the past few days. There were still patches of it about the estate. He had to report back for ten o'clock. He should get back in time for a shower and a couple of hours sleep. He started the engine and drove back towards the Forth Road Bridge. His whole body was shaking with the comedown from the adrenaline rush. It felt like a drug withdrawal. He wondered if they'd all feel like this or if it was just the first. He put on a CD.

He was driving at some speed now. It wasn't long before he was on English roads again. He was somewhere in Northumberland. The road was empty. Desolate. The CD was booming out in the darkness. An album of gangsta rap. He listened to the rappers telling him how hard they were and how hard he was. How he should smoke more weed. He agreed. He took the plump spliff from the ashtray and pressed down the cigarette lighter. In a matter of seconds it clicked back. He took it, the coil of metal glowing orange and pink, and lit the spliff. He breathed the pungent flower heads deep into his lungs. It tasted good. There were no lights along this stretch. There had been some cat's eyes but they'd finished a mile or two back. Just the headlamps from the car to show him the road. It was quite narrow. There was no hard shoulder. Now and again there was a passing point. To his left there were mountains. He passed several signs warning him of falling rocks. He looked up the side of the mountain range – almost vertical scree. To his right was a sheer drop. Just a swamp of darkness. It was perfectly possible to imagine that he was staring into an abyss.

He slowed down a little. The spliff was starting to kick in and he thought he better take it easy. He was only a third into the thing when he decided he'd had enough. His head was in bits. The music was drifting in and out, slowing down and then quickening as though the motor were faulty. He could feel great waves of intensity wooze across his body. He gripped the steering wheel tight. He shifted down into third gear. It was like driving on wet putty. Everything felt soft: the road surface, the foot pedals, his chair. The steering wheel was slipping through his fingers.

He stared at the road in front, the two eyes of light the headlamps made on the tarmac. He had to tense his eyelids to keep them open. So heavy. Like lifting weights. He stared into the eyes of light, the shadows and shapes they made. There were two focused spots surrounded by paler, more diffuse areas. The light surrounding them made a face. The darkness of night made the outline of a human head.

He was looking into the eyes of Chris Obassi. The dark fiery eyes. Cruel, relentless, unforgiving. He was watching Chris's face take shape on the surface of the road in front of him. It was Chris Obassi. The same shaven lump of skull, the ears, the square jaw and huge neck. He could see his mouth and nose. Everything. All his features became clearly detailed. A massive projection of Chris Obassi directly in his sight. It must have been ten, twenty feet, in height.

The mouth opened and Chris Obassi began to talk to Andy.

Well done, Andy, I'm proud of what you did today. I knew you had it in you. Didn't I tell you? You just needed the fire in you. We'll make a salesman out of you yet, get you out of those Burton's suits.

He didn't dare tell him he'd got the suit from a charity shop. The shirts, the tie and the shoes also.

Will it always feel this good, Chris?

The massive face of Chris Obassi creased and the night was filled with his deep timbrous laugh.

It feels good, it always feels good. But you've got to cut that out. He nodded to Andy, indicating the extinguished spliff. That's for losers. If you're going to be a salesman you need to keep your head clear. Always one step in front of the customer. You understand me, boy?

Yes, Chris...

He had slowed down now to less than 20 mph, barely able even to keep the car on the road at this speed as it snaked through the mountains. The blackness of the mountains took on a sinister tone. He could see the road in front, see the dark nothingness and the mountains, but he was struggling to grip and co-ordinate the steering wheel. He was driving towards the mountain. He could see it coming straight at him but he couldn't feel the wheel.

A split second before crashing he came round enough to turn the car back on course.

What did I tell you, boy? No good will come of it...

He was nodding in agreement but he'd lost control again. This time he was heading for the sheer drop to his right. He tried to grip the wheel but it was no use. Again a split second between him and death as he grappled and fumbled with the wheel. He was terrified. He couldn't keep his eyes open. It just wasn't possible. He had to let them shut for a second before opening them. But when he did they were lead weights and he couldn't find the strength to open them again. This time two seconds and another near miss with the mountain. He was only doing 10 mph but it was more than he was able to control in his state of inebriation.

He closed his lids again. What relief, what bliss. Four seconds. Then he forced them open again half a yard before the edge of the road. If he didn't stop he would die. He would either be buried under a tonne of scree or hurtle over the edge of the cliff. He looked for somewhere to pull up but there was nowhere. Perhaps if he got some air, he would wake up a bit. It was two o'clock. He pressed the button above his head. The sunroof was still a novelty – he'd never driven in a car with an electric sunroof. He heard the motor whir as the sunroof opened. He pressed it again and it whirred shut. He liked this game, the neatness of the machine, the hissing sound of the mechanism.

Then, whoosh. The glass panel had disappeared. It must have popped off. Fuck. He'd only had the car a week and already he'd bust it. What would Chris say? He stopped the car in the middle of the road and climbed out. It was bitterly cold and there was snow collected in piles by the side. He walked up and down a stretch of about a hundred yards, kneeling down every so often, digging into the snow to see if he could find the glass panel. Why when everything was going right did something always have to fuck up? It was nowhere. He could be here all night groping in the snow and still he'd be no closer. The glass was see-through, it wasn't even as though he could look for its outline. He almost laughed. It was insane: looking for a sheet of glass in the snow in the middle of the night. He made his way back to the car.

He had a thought – perhaps it was still attached by the electrical wires and was hanging off the roof. Worth a go. In his stoned state it was a struggle to get a grip, but eventually he managed to climb onto the roof of the car and make his way on all fours to the hole at the front. Nothing. Not even a rough edge where it had snapped. It must have come clean off. How odd. He got back into the car. He'd come round a bit but was still stoned. He could tell by the way the music sounded. He pressed the button to see if he could discover how it came off, and there it was, hissing back, closing the gap – the glass panel. It dawned on him, of course, the sunroof folds back into the body of the roof of the car. He felt such relief that he laughed. His voice sounded small. He played with the new toy for a bit before settling on half-shut half-open. He began driving again, still chuckling at his own stupidity.

He made a bit of distance but it was no use, he just couldn't keep his eyes open. He kept experiencing snatches of sleep. Bliss. Before his unconscious woke him up again to be confronted with his near-death. How many times he did this he wasn't certain, but as soon as he came across a passing point he pulled up and switched off the engine. He'd have to sleep here until it was light and the drug had worn off. He took his overcoat from the back seat. It was another charity shop acquisition. He wondered what Chris would have to say about it. He'd already called him a tramp. But he didn't care. In truth, money had never meant that much to him, not on the scale it did for the other salesman. He wasn't bothered about designer labels, it all seemed a bit of a con really. And besides, it was a good overcoat – wool and mink mix. He put his chair back as far as it would go and wrapped himself in the snug overcoat. He closed his eyes, his mind still whirring with the day's events. The shoe box of money was behind his chair.

He was just nodding off when he heard a rumbling, faint at first but building. A thunderous groan somewhere in the distance. He listened to it get louder and louder. The sound building so much that it shook the car. He could feel its hum resonate deep inside him. His whole body was vibrating with the noise. The build-up seemed to go on forever. The vibrations in his body becoming stronger and stronger. Then he saw a flash of light in his rear-view mirror. He turned to look out the back window. He could see a lorry, a huge juggernaut, making its way towards him at rapid speed. He panicked – what if it didn't see him? He turned his lights onto full beam. His body was vibrating so much now it was painful. He hugged himself and clenched all his muscles. As the truck approached he could feel his stomach about to explode. He was tensing each one of his muscles as tight as he could. His arms twisted in an embrace – holding himself together.

As the lorry came even closer it shook the whole car violently. It drove so close to the body that it seemed to brush it. As it overtook it seemed to burst from his stomach, as though he were giving birth to it. He screamed out in agony. So painful, his limbs being ripped open. Once it had gone he checked himself, made sure he was in one piece. Just about. He lay back again and closed his eyes. His heart was a fist punching the inside of his chest, but he could feel it diminish in intensity. He relaxed once again. It must be the sensi. He'd had mad rushes like that before, but never so strong, never so violent.

He was drifting off again, his body sinking into sleep, when he heard the distant rumble once more. His sat up and braced himself. This second truck if anything was even worse. The agonising anticipation, now that he knew what he must suffer, made it so much more unbearable. There was a third and a fourth. Each one seemed stronger than the last, faster, bigger, more violent. He was absolutely worn out from tensing his muscles. He started up the engine. He'd risk the drive back.

He got to the office in plenty of time. He'd managed a couple of hours kip at home. A shower and some breakfast. He was clutching the shoe box under one arm, holding his briefcase in the other. He said good morning to the receptionist. She returned his smile. He felt restored and triumphant. The bosses all came out to shake his hand, pat him on the back. Congratulate him. Chris disappeared with the box into Trevor's office. Andy got himself a coffee from the machine and sat down in the waiting room. A few minutes later Chris reappeared and ushered Andy into the office. His blank expression giving away no emotion.

Inside the office there was a chair in the middle of the room. Chris pointed to it: Sit down. He did. Chris went first. So where is it?

What? He genuinely didn't know what he was talking about.

Come off it, Andy, you know.

He didn't.

The money, Andy. Stop messing about, just hand it over.

What do you mean? I gave you the money, it's in the shoe box. He looked over at the box on the desk. Its lid off, contents spilled.

All of it, Andy. We want all the money?

What? I don't get this, I watched Mr Kirkpatrick count it all out, watched Mrs Kirkpatrick load it all up. What's the matter, isn't it all there?

There's only nine hundred and fifty – fifty quid is missing.

Well I've not got it.

Both Chris and Trevor stood over him staring, not saying anything. Then Trevor started.

Ok, Andy, we've all done it. If you give it us back now we'll forget all about it.

But I haven't got it, really I haven't.

Look, Andy, I'm getting mad now. Now, you're a bit of a wide boy, we all know that, I interviewed you, remember? There's nothing wrong with that. In this sort of business it's an advantage. But you don't steal off us, you steal off the customer. Have you got that?

Look, I know that, do you think if I was going to nick some money off you I'd just take the fifty? No, I'd rob the lot. I'm getting commission off that, why the hell would I take some of it out?

Chris again now: Look, Andy, we've all been tempted. That's the job, you work on your own. You're trusted. There's no other way round it. We take that risk. Now I'm warning you, Andy, we know you're made up, your first sale and all that, you're on a bit of a high, bound to be, but I'm warning you, you've got ten seconds to hand that over and then we'll search you, and if we find it on you we're gonna put your head on the block – have you got that?

Go ahead, search me, I've nothing to hide, I've not got it.

Chris started the countdown, Ten, nine, eight... three, two, one. Then Trevor told Andy to stand up and Chris and Trevor searched him. They got him to empty his pockets. Car keys, chewing gum, loose change, but no notes. He put everything back. It was Trevor's turn now.

I'll tell you what we'll do. Me and Chris will leave the room. We'll leave that money there on the desk, and we'll leave the office empty till dinnertime. Now, if at dinnertime we come back and find the box with all the money then we'll say no more about it. Understand?

I've had enough of this. Why don't you just ring the customer? Ring Mr and Mrs Kirkpatrick and ask them. It's probably fallen on the floor or something.

We can't do that, Andy. What sort of business do you think we're running here? Ring the customer? And say what? That one of our employees is a thieving little toe-rag? Or we say we don't trust the customer to keep their side of the deal? How will that look?

Just tell them you've only got nine hundred and fifty quid and would they mind seeing if they've got the other fifty lying around somewhere. If they've not then it's no problem. If they've not I'll give you the fifty out of my wages if you like. I'm telling you for the last time I've not got it, they have.

He stood up and stared at them both in turn. Finally Trevor nodded to Chris, Go on Chris, give them a ring, they've signed the contract, they can't back down now. Chris left the office. Andy and Trevor sat down. Trevor at his desk, Andy on the chair in the middle of the room. Trevor took the money and started loading it back in the box.

I'm warning you, Andy, that money better be where you say it is.

Andy said nothing. Just stared.

Chris came back into the room. You're in luck, it'd slipped under the rug, Mrs Kirkpatrick found it this morning when she was cleaning. She was going to give us a ring.

Trevor nodded and turned to Andy. OK, Andy, looks like you win this one. See Chris outside, he'll give you your next assignment. Andy was stunned. He'd expected at the very least, an apology.

His next job was Poole in Dorset. It was now eleven o'clock. He had an appointment for five o'clock. There was no way he could make it. He had a proper address this time, however, and a phone number. He supposed he could always ring nearer the time, explain he was running late. He got down there by about 5.30 p.m., bought an A to Z. He wasn't that far off. He'd make it for six, no need to ring if he was only an hour late.

Thirty minutes later he was pulling up outside the property. It was a beautiful detached house overlooking the coast. Four storeys with balconies on the top floor and a built-in garage on the bottom. The driveway was immense, stretching in a huge curve around the grounds. And even better, it was tatty concrete, all split and cracked with gaps where bits had gone missing. Should be a cinch.

How much resin-bonded driveway was there? Must be about £20,000 worth. That was £2,000 in commission. He felt giddy. He'd never so much as even sniffed that kind of money. He straightened up his tie in the mirror, draped the camera around his neck. His head was spinning with ways to spend the money. He hadn't received a single penny yet, it was all worked out at the end of the second month. He made his way up the ruined path and swung the huge brass knocker.

A man, mid-fifties, came to the door. He was wearing a dinner suit and a black bow tie.

Yes, can I help you?

Stoneway, you rang to enquire about our driveways. I'm a surveyor and was just pass—

A woman appeared behind him. Who is it, dear?

A man from Stoneway. I thought you'd sorted that driveway out?

She budged passed him. I have, dear. Some man was round this morning, I did what you said, went for block paving. I'm sorry about this, sorry to bring you out here for nothing, I should have rang, but to be honest I didn't think you'd show. The woman on the phone said you'd pop round if you were passing. I didn't understand it as a formal appointment.

No, it's not, that's right... Can I just take five minutes of your time? I appreciate you've already decided on block paving, but I think it's only fair to warn you that it's not really suitable for the kind of expansive driveway you have. I'm only giving you the benefit of my experience. I don't want you to make the wrong choice, that's all.

Look, I'm sorry, I am really, but my wife has told you we've already made a decision.

That's right, dear, I've signed the contract this morning, I had to do it there and then, the man said he could use our driveway for one of those 'before and after' shots, only had one space left, was driving back to Birmingham, had to get it all finalised.

You did right, dear.

Oh, I know, I'm rather pleased with myself. He took 25% off the cost – it was a bargain.

Andy's heart slumped down into his stomach. He had an awful gnawing feeling in the pit of his gut.

You say you've signed the contract?

Yes, this morning.

You've really signed the contract?

I've just told you haven't I, what's the matter with you? Are you deaf?

But, but... I've come from Manchester...

I thought you said you were just passing. What is all this? Are you trying to pull a fast one?

Looks like you did the right thing, darling, this Stoneway firm seem like a lot a cowboys to me...

You don't understand, I'm not a salesman, I'm a surveyor, you can set it and forget it, use it and abuse it... Absolutely guaranteed, non-slip... Resin...

Look, young man, I don't know what you're up to but you'd better go. We haven't time for all this nonsense. Now, we've given you a perfectly reasonable explanation...

But, but... Would you mind if I could just use your phone?

Use our phone? Good heavens! What on earth for?

I need to make a quick phone call.

No, absolutely not. There's a phone box down the road, you can use that, now clear off.

I'll give you the money for—

I'll not tell you again.

The man closed the door in Andy's face. It felt almost as if he'd been punched. He turned around and hobbled back down the drive. It was bitterly cold. The ice was biting at his ankles. His knuckles clasping his briefcase were stinging with the frost. He got back into his car. He watched the man and woman leave their house and get into their vehicle. It was a nice motor – expensive. He watched them drive off into the distance, all dolled up for an evening of entertainment – fine wine and good food. They didn't notice his Fiat Tempra parked on the opposite side of the road, its simple black shape unobtrusive in the shadow of their home.

He stared out at the coast. The gulls were screaming. Every part of his body felt cold. He took his coat from the back and wrapped it around himself. What was he going to do? What now? He couldn't go back.

He stared out at the sea, the grey waves and the flashes of light. The bright ice of sky. He looked at the sand, the tiny insignificant grains. The tide was coming in, lapping and frothing at the edge of the beach. The gulls were overhead now, their cries deafening. He watched the waves, advancing and retreating. He watched the water crash against the rocks. The spray catching the bleached glare of the sun. The tear-like drops returning to the ocean. He was shivering. He hugged his woollen overcoat and closed his eyes. He didn't know why it came to him then, but the image he had in his mind was that of the geese, their mouths forced open and metal funnels shoved deep into their gullets. Rows and rows of them, clamped in place. Their eyes staring out in distress. The image went on. There were warehouses full of them. As far as the eye could see. He opened his eyes again and focussed on the ocean. It was all he could see around him. It went on and on until his eyes couldn't see anymore. There was just a general grey where he thought the horizon must be, that merged with the sky. He put the key in the ignition and started the engine.

It was early morning when he got back to Manchester. The sun had yet to rise. He parked the car in the Stoneway car park and put the key through the letterbox in the front door. He began the long walk back to his flat along the river Irwell. But then he turned round and returned to the letterbox. He opened his briefcase and took out a pen and a piece of paper. He wrote, 'You can fuck your job' and posted it through the hole.

HOME

"In every dream home a heartache." Bryan Ferry

84

just waving

The woman was standing by the window watching the street below. The cars. The people. It was always a busy road. There was a bus stop with two shops either side: a newsagent and an off-licence. The rain had stopped and an old man was walking round a puddle that had appeared where the pavement was cracked. There were potholes in the road, marked with white paint. The cars dodged the potholes but occasionally one was unlucky and there was a thunk sound as the wheel sunk into the hole. They used to come and fill the holes, but these days they just left them, or painted a white circle around them. That was the best you could hope for. A bus pulled up and three people got off. Two people waiting at the stop got on. The doors closed. The bus pulled away. She could waste hours like this. But today she was looking for a black car with a scratch up one side and a sticker in the window which said, *more revs per life.*

The boy was sitting at the table drawing a picture. He'd done the house and the tree and the cat. He was saving the man till last. It was hard to draw people. To make the picture look like the person you were drawing. If they had glasses it was easy. Or a big nose. Or curly hair. He was good at drawing curly hair. He liked the flow of the crayon as he twisted it round and round.

Sometimes he would forget that he was drawing the hair and he would just keep on going, curling round and round so it looked like the head of the person was exploding. He was trying to draw his dad. But he found it hard to draw him. His dad had a thin face and short brown hair. All his features were normal. No big nose or big ears or sticky out teeth. No glasses. No beard or moustache. Nothing. He wanted to finish it. His dad was on his way. He hadn't seen him for a long time. He wanted to give him the picture.

The woman went into the kitchen and opened the fridge. She took out the sandwich box and a bottle of fizzy drink. She didn't let him have fizzy drink but today was different. She'd made him his favourite sandwiches, tomato sauce. He wasn't allowed these usually. She tried to feed him healthy food. She took a banana from the bowl. Unzipped his rucksack, loaded it up with the sandwich box, fizzy drink and the banana. It was already going brown and she knew he wouldn't eat a banana if there was any brown on but maybe he wouldn't notice. She had told him time and time again that the banana grew sweeter the older it got, but it was no use, he said the brown bits were bad. Even when the banana was free of brown bits, he would never eat the whole thing. He would always leave a bit. He did this with all his food. She wasn't allowed as a child to leave food, she got told off. But she tried not to enforce this rule now. It was important to do things differently.

The boy was colouring in the T-shirt of the man who was standing between the house and the tree, next to the cat. He was using red crayon even though he'd never seen his dad in a red T-shirt. He wanted blue, but he'd ran out of blue because he'd used it all colouring in the sky. Maybe his dad would wear a red T-shirt when he gave him the picture. He would see himself with the red T-shirt on and like it. Then he'd go to a shop and buy a red T-shirt. He wondered if they would go shopping together. The last time he saw his dad was over two years ago and he had been wearing a blue T-shirt. They had gone shopping together. They had gone to a toy shop and bought some toys. Then they had gone to McDonald's. His dad had bought him a burger and a milkshake and some fries. Then they had gone to the park and walked round the lake. He'd wanted a go on the boats. There were boats you could hire, rowing boats and ones you pedalled. But his dad said he couldn't afford it so instead they had sat on a bench and watched another boy row with his father round the island in the middle.

The woman took the bag and came back into the living room. She placed it on the table next to the picture. Don't forget your bag, she said. I've finished, he said, holding up his picture. That's very good. I like the colours. Your dad will love it.

Has he still got a cat? the boy asked.

I don't know. I expect so.

Do you think he'll take me to his house?

I don't know.

Why can't I sleep there?

I've gone over that before. You are going out for the day then he is bringing you back. That's the arrangement. Don't spoil it.

But I want to sleep over. I want to see the cat.

You can't sleep over.

Why not?

Look, we've been through this.

Please.

Don't. I haven't got the strength.

The boy put the picture down and sat back in his chair. Eventually he said, I hate you. The woman turned away. She didn't want him to see the tears pricking her eyes. She wiped them away with the back of her hand. Then she wiped her hand on her top. She looked at the scars between her knuckles and her wrist. Cigarette burns.

Where is he, Mum?

He'll be here any minute, she said. Traffic is bad. There might have been an accident.

Has Dad had an accident?

Not your dad. Another accident. It slows down the traffic.

Why, Mum? Why does it slow the traffic down?

It just does, alright.

She went to the window again and peered out at the cars and buses. The vehicles were moving. There were just too many on the road. That was the problem. Too many cars, too many buses, too many people. It was people that were the problem. They were like rats. Breeding all the time and consuming everything. She'd heard he had a new girlfriend. She'd bumped into Siobhan in Tescos.

Oh, fancy seeing you here. Not seen you for ages. How is everything? Have you heard? He's got out.

No, she hadn't heard. He'd been released early for good behaviour. Good behaviour. That was a joke. But he could put the charm on when he wanted to. Like when they first met. That big smile he had. That laugh. Like a boy's laugh. A laugh like that was attractive. She hadn't seen the anger inside of him then.

What time is it, Mum?

She looked at her watch. He was half an hour late now.

He won't be long, love.

But–

Like I say, probably stuck in traffic. Why don't you get your coat and your gloves so that you're ready for him when he comes?

The boy got up and went over to the cupboard where the coats were kept. His coat was hung up on the leg of the ironing board. He had to stretch up to reach it. He found his gloves in the basket on top of the dryer where the hats and scarves and gloves were kept.

It's cold out there, his mum said. So get your scarf too.

I don't want my scarf.

Look, it's brass monkeys. Please. Do as you're told.

What's brass monkeys?

It just means it is very cold.

But why brass monkeys? Are brass monkeys cold?

She had no idea where the phrase came from. It was just something she had repeated without ever really thinking about. So many things in her life were like that. Just taken for granted. Never really understood. She looked around the room. At the television, and the light switch. She didn't understand how any of it worked. What was electricity? How did the images get on her telly? The phone in her bag was an even greater mystery.

The boy was unzipping his rucksack.

What are you doing?

I want to put this picture in.

Better to hold it, she said. You'll only crease it.

I want to put it in.

You'll ruin it. Just give it to him when he gets here. It's too big to go in there.

The boy gave up. He put the picture back down and re-zipped his bag.

Where is he, Mum? Where is Dad?

She looked at her watch again. Forty minutes late. He was always late. Even on their first date. She'd stood by the market stalls waiting for him for nearly an hour. Why had she waited? She wouldn't have waited for anyone else that long. It had surprised her at the time, that she was prepared to wait so long. And how nervous she was. Then he appeared. Looking all cool and unflustered.

You're late, she'd said, but he'd just shrugged.

Yeah, sorry about that. Got held up. I'm here now though, where do you want to go?

She hadn't minded, just out of the cold somewhere. He took her hand in his and gave it a squeeze. His hand was warm. Her hand was cold.

They had gone to a bar she'd never been to before full of old men.

It's like a morgue in here, she had said as a joke.

I like it, he said, some right characters. What do you want to drink?

He bought himself a pint and her a half pint and they had sat and laughed at the people he pointed out. He knew them. Knew their stories.

See that bloke there stood at the bar? They call him Cherry Blossom.

Why's that?

You know cherry blossom shoe polish?

She nodded.

He used to put it on his head.

What for?

To cover a bald patch. Until one day, he had an argument with this bloke. This bloke took out his lighter and set fire to it. It's flammable, shoe polish, did you know that? It's got turps in it and other flammable stuff. So he's stood there with this little fire on his head. Didn't notice at first. Then he screams. Picks up his pint pot and pours it over his head. Dead funny. You had to be there.

The phone in her bag buzzed. It was on the sofa. She took it out. A text message: I'm outside. She went to the window. Not the car she was expecting. Suppose he would have sold it before he went inside. No sense in keeping it. He was parked up by the house in a grey car. He stared out of the window and they made eye contact. He nodded without smiling. She turned away.

He's here, she said. Come on, get your coat on.

She helped the boy zip up the front all the way to his chin. She wrapped his scarf around his neck. She helped him with his gloves. She took the rucksack and helped him carry it on his back.

Here, she said, don't forget this.

She handed him the picture. She walked him to the front door, opened it, and gave him a kiss.

Have a good time, she said. Be good for your dad. Don't make him angry. I love you, she said.

But he was already running towards the car. She watched them drive away, waving goodbye. The car was turning up another street. Then it was gone. And she was still waving.

home

It were dark when I woke up. There were two empty bottles of wine by the bed. I stared at the slit of light under the door, looking for movement. Nothing. I closed my eyes and tried to get back to sleep. I were sinking back when I heard a bang. Blood rushed through my veins. Heart pumping. I thought about getting up, but I were naked under the sheets. So I lay in the dark, eyes wide open. I heard a floorboard creak. Then I saw the slit of light under the door darken. Someone was outside my room. My heart were pumping so hard it hurt my chest. The handle turning. The door opening. The slit of light growing. There were someone coming into the room. And now I could make out the silhouette of a person. Large shoulders, short hair. A man.

What to do? Pretend to be asleep. What would he do? He'd have a walk around, see if there was anything worth stealing and then go away, wouldn't he? I closed my eyes tight and stayed as still as I could. He was entering the room. He was tiptoeing towards me. The weight of his body as he sits down on the bed only inches from the pillow.

I know you're awake, Sarah.

He knew my name. I tried to breathe. I were frozen in terror.

Open your eyes and look at me.

I were trapped. There were nothing I could do. As I opened my eyes, I could see him sitting a few feet away. His back straight. He were staring into my eyes. He were naked and his hair was dripping wet. There were drops of water all over his body, but I knew who it was. Michael?

He were shivering. For almost a minute it seemed, he just sat there. I wanted to hold him but something stopped me. I didn't know where I was, he said. It was dark. I was looking for a way out but I couldn't see in front of me. It was such a strange feeling. How did I know it was him when he'd gone eighteen years ago? How could I tell when he were a baby then and now a man? But I knew, I just knew. I pulled back the covers. Michael, you're cold. Come under the sheets. As he climbs in I wrap the blanket around him. It's ok, I say. You're home now.

the shivering man

On the subject of lodgers Ruth was insistent: it had to be a man. Vikram wanted to know why, but all Ruth would say was, Because, just because. Vikram didn't want to argue with Ruth but he didn't like the idea of another man in the house, using the bathroom, watching Ruth hang out her underwear on the line. He preferred the idea of a female lodger. Still, it wasn't worth falling out over. They'd been together for over five years now and not one altercation. Other couples argued, other couples fought, but not Ruth and Vikram.

Ruth and Vikram had lived in a Victorian terrace on the main street of the village for about two years. Ruth worked as a nurse on an oncology ward of the local hospital. Vikram was finishing the final year of his PhD. He was writing about the cult of Roman Mithraism. Ruth was ten years older than Vikram, though didn't look it, and they were, by any measure, very happy together. Only recently, they'd been having financial problems. Nursing didn't pay well, and Vikram had had to give up his part-time job to focus on his thesis. Getting a lodger was Ruth's idea.

He can stay in the attic, we won't even know he's there most of the time.

I don't know. I'm not sure.

They'd discussed it for several weeks, until a series of bills had brought

Vikram to a point of submission. They'd worked together on the wording of the advert and agreed to charge £350 a month excluding bills. Ruth wanted to specify a non-smoker, but Vikram persuaded her that this was them enforcing their own lifestyle on others, and Ruth conceded, if the lodger confined his smoking habits to his own room.

The next day Vikram bought a massive tin of one-coat magnolia paint. Together they painted the room. The day after they cleaned and hoovered. Ruth found a rug rolled up behind the stairs, which they'd bought last year, but hadn't gone with anything when they had laid it out on the living room floor. In the neutral space of the attic, it looked vibrant and appealing. Vikram took the lamp from the spare room and plugged it in next to the bed. Its light was warm and soothing, and made the room cosy. They hung a few pictures up and opened the skylight to air the room out.

The first respondent was an arborist with inflamed skin, who wore a black Breton cap. He hadn't made eye contact and had mumbled. He was softly spoken, painfully shy and, they both felt, potentially a concern. He was the sort of bloke you'd read about in the paper, who'd lived with his mother for thirty years, before shooting up the local infant school.

The second candidate was a middle-aged man, who had recently split up with his wife and who said he worked nights, so would be 'no bovver'. He had a heavy, rasping breathing pattern, and kept spitting into a handkerchief: 'so sorry, huh huh.' When Ruth closed the door behind him, they had given each other a look: he wasn't suitable.

They had to run the advert for another week and they were getting desperate, when one Tuesday morning, about 11am, there was a knock at the door. He was a man in his early twenties and he said his name was Alasdair. He worked as a car salesman at a local Rover showroom. He was polite and dressed in a sober suit. He was tall and wiry with wavy blonde hair that he'd gelled to his scalp. There was something very easy in his manner. He made eye contact with them both and had a cheeky smile. They hadn't discussed it. He was the one for them.

He'd moved in on the Saturday. Vikram had helped him carry the boxes up two flights of stairs. He didn't have much stuff: a few books, a laptop, a Bluetooth speaker. He had a wide screen television and a DVD player. The rest was mostly clothes.

Where's the bedding?

Vikram was walking across the attic with the last of the boxes. Alasdair was stood by the bed.

I'm sorry?

When I came on Tuesday, there was bedding.

Vikram explained that the bedding had just been for show. The room hadn't looked right without bedding on the bed. Alasdair explained that he'd assumed the bedding was for him. He didn't have any of his own.

Not to worry, you can borrow it for now.

Vikram had fetched the bedding and he'd helped Alasdair make the bed.

Are you ok then?

Alasdair nodded. He was fine. Vikram hung about for a bit before popping the question about the deposit. He hated talking about money, it always felt so grasping and vulgar, but Ruth had instructed him to get the cash immediately.

Sorry to ask, but have you got the deposit?

Alasdair had agreed to pay £350 refundable deposit, plus a month's rent in advance, totalling seven hundred pounds. But he seemed to have forgotten. He looked at Vikram blankly.

The deposit for the room, and the rent. Seven hundred quid we said, remember?

Vikram shuffled about on his feet nervously. He put his hands behind his back, not quite knowing what to do with them.

Oh, that deposit. Alasdair gave Vikram a warm smile, Of course, no worries... Only, they're a bit late with my commission this month. Should have it by Monday.

He smiled at Vikram again.

Oh, right, I see. Well, that's fine. Monday will be fine then.

Vikram welcomed Alasdair into his house, I hope you'll be happy here, and if there's any problem, just ask me... Or Ruth.

They shook hands, and Vikram left Alasdair to do his unpacking.

When Monday arrived, Ruth urged Vikram to get the money off Alasdair as soon as he came home from work. So when he heard Alasdair's key in the front door that evening, he was up on his feet straight away.

Good day at work?

Yes thanks.

Settling in ok?

Yes thanks.

They stood in the hallway. There was an awkward pause as Vikram plucked up the courage to pop the question.

Did you get your commission then?

Alasdair shook his head slowly and deliberately, Bloody boss. He was in a meeting all day.

Oh, I see. Not to worry. Tomorrow will do.

He moved to let Alasdair pass and then went back to Ruth. She wasn't pleased, but he assured her, they'd get it the next day, there was nothing to worry about.

When he failed again on Tuesday, Ruth was visibly annoyed. She pinched her forehead – a gesture which made Vikram uneasy. He was to insist. He wasn't to take no for an answer. On both Wednesday and Thursday Vikram tried again, but his labour bore no fruit. Listening to Vikram's flustered story on Friday evening, Ruth snapped. She'd have to do it herself. Why was it that whenever anything needed doing, it was always her who ended up doing it? Vikram tried to smooth things over, but she wouldn't listen. Their argument was interrupted by the sound of Alasdair's key in the front door.

Ruth didn't even wait for him to shut the door.

Now listen, I want that money or there's going to be trouble.

Alasdair seemed taken aback. He reached into the inside pocket of his suit jacket, Of course you can. I've got it for you here.

He took out the money and handed it over.

My boss has been away all week. Sorry about that.

It was all there. Ruth walked into the living room, holding the wad of notes triumphantly. Vikram was a little annoyed. Alasdair had promised him yesterday that he'd have the money today, so there was no need for Ruth to take the credit. He'd been handling it.

Ruth walked across. She gave him a hug and a kiss, Sorry love, I shouldn't have doubted you, I was just getting a bit tetchy.

Vikram seemed to cheer up. He kissed her neck, It's ok.

That night, they went out and spent seventy of it on a meal and a few beers down the local pub. Vikram was to put the rest in their joint account first thing Monday morning.

The first few weeks things went pretty smooth. They hardly saw Alasdair, as he was at work during the day, and would be out most nights. But then, fifteen days after he had moved in, Alasdair had come home at two in the afternoon looking upset about something. Ruth was in the kitchen making Vikram and herself a drink when Alasdair entered with his head down and his shoulders hunched forward.

Everything ok?

No.

You're home early.

I've been sacked.

Ruth told him she was sorry to hear that, but that a bright young kid like him would soon find another sales job. She made him a cup of tea. She took Vikram's through to the living room. Vikram agreed with Ruth that it was nothing to worry about. You could always get a job in sales. Especially if you were young like Alasdair.

Three days later, Vikram bumped into Alasdair in the hallway. He was coming out of the bathroom and was now evidently going out for the evening. Vikram said hello to him and they parted company, only Vikram noticed that Alasdair smelled familiar. In fact, he stunk of Ruth's favourite perfume. He was sure of it.

He went into the bathroom, and sure enough, the bottle of Eau D'Issey was nearly empty. It had been half full. Alasdair had sprayed practically half a bottle on himself. Vikram's first feeling was one of anger, but then this was mingled with a feeling of confusion. What was Alasdair doing wearing Ruth's perfume? He decided not to tell Ruth. She would, understandably, go spare and cause a big scene. He decided instead to tackle Alasdair about it in the morning, by having a quiet word with him.

Alasdair didn't come home that night, or the next night, so it was several days before the chance arose for Vikram to discuss the matter of the perfume with Alasdair. Ruth was out at the shops, and he could hear

Alasdair playing his music upstairs, so he knew he was in. It was now or never. Vikram mounted the stairs and approached the attic door. He listened for a moment, before knocking. Alasdair beckoned him to come up.

It was the first time Vikram had been into the room since he helped Alasdair move in with the boxes, so he was surprised to see the pictures from the walls were missing. But then, perhaps that wasn't so surprising, the work of Henri Rousseau wasn't to everyone's taste. He supposed he'd stored them somewhere. But he was also surprised about the general appearance of the room. There were beer cans and pizza boxes everywhere. There were several ashtrays on the floor, that were piled up with the extinguished ends of hand rolled cigarettes. Vikram didn't even know Alasdair smoked. He hadn't mentioned it when they had interviewed him. Still, he supposed it was none of his business, he and Ruth had agreed on that.

Sorry to disturb you, Alasdair.

That's alright.

Alasdair was lying on his bed in his boxer shorts. He was listening to some heavy rock whilst flicking through a magazine.

I just wondered if I could have a quick chat.

Alasdair put the magazine down, Of course. What about?

Vikram came a little closer to the bed, Well, it was just that I noticed you were wearing Ruth's perfume the other night –

He was interrupted by Alasdair before he had chance to finish his sentence, What you on about?

A few nights ago, you were going out and you were wearing Eau D'Issey, Ruth's favourite scent, and I wouldn't bother you but –

Alasdair interrupted again, What you talking about?

There's no point denying it, Alasdair, I saw the bottle.

Alasdair looked blankly back. Vikram explained that he wasn't angry with him, and that he hadn't told Ruth, but that he wasn't to do it again. It was an easy mistake to make, probably thought it was aftershave, but that it was very expensive, and if Ruth had caught him... Well, he didn't say. He looked at Alasdair as if to suggest it would be catastrophic.

Alasdair was indignant. He didn't know what Vikram was talking about, and he didn't like being accused of something he hadn't done. Vikram said a few more words, got nowhere and left the room. He'd felt a little sick.

Perhaps he'd made a mistake. Perhaps he hadn't noticed the level of liquid in the bottle going down. Perhaps he'd imagined the smell. He'd experienced that before, though usually it was just before going to sleep. He'd be dropping off and he'd detect a very distinctive smell, usually from his childhood. It was best, therefore, to give Alasdair the benefit of the doubt.

The next night, Ruth and Vikram had been awoken at three in the morning by the sound of thumping music, shouting and laughing. The noise was coming from the attic. Ruth pushed Vikram out of bed and told him to investigate. He put on his towelling dressing gown and went into the hallway. He stood by the attic door. He placed his ear against the wood. He could hear Alasdair, and also a woman's voice. What should he do? They hadn't mentioned bringing people back, so it was unfair to impose the rule now. The music had quietened down. He went to the toilet.

Walking back along the corridor towards his bedroom, he was disturbed by the sight of Alasdair and a girl, of no more than sixteen or seventeen, stood in the hallway. They were both naked. They looked startled when they saw Vikram, but then turned to each other and giggled. The girl had a pierced nipple and a tattoo of a dragon below her belly button. Alasdair had a wound across his torso and was bleeding, although he didn't seem to be in any pain. Vikram noticed that both Alasdair and the girl seemed to be acting strange, and that their pupils were dilated.

He made an embarrassed gesture and then walked past them, into his bedroom. He was relieved to close the door behind him. He wished there was a lock on their door. He made a mental note to get one the next day. Ruth appeared to be asleep. He took off his dressing gown and sidled in next to her. Her body was warm and smooth. He put his hand on her stomach. It felt reassuring.

Ruth worked a late shift on Wednesdays and wouldn't get back till gone ten. Sometimes, on those nights, Vikram would have his tea down the pub and wash it down with a few real ales. It was a decent pub, with proper hand pumps and a blackboard with usually three or four guest ales chalked up on it. Dave and Barbara, the landlord and landlady, were pleasant enough, and always said hello. He'd got into the habit of asking Dave's advice about which beer to choose.

Light or dark mate?

Depending on his mood, Vikram would opt for a dark or light ale, and then Dave would give him his recommendation. Only tonight, Vikram was surprised when Dave blanked him. He looked over to Barbara, but she turned away too. He was puzzled and disturbed. He looked at the blackboard. He made his choice and was served by a barmaid.

He didn't stay the usual three hours. Instead, he finished his drink and walked back home. He would get some chips on the way and watch some telly. As he walked, he felt more and more aggrieved by Dave and Barbara's treatment of him. What was that all about, he wondered? And what had he done to deserve it? He tried to shrug it off, but each time he did, it loomed larger and more vivid in his mind.

When he opened his front door, he heard voices. They were coming from the living room. One of the voices was Alasdair's. He closed the door behind him. He had to play this one right. They hadn't actually said to Alasdair that the living room was out of bounds, they merely suggested it. Perhaps it was their fault and not Alasdair's. He approached the living room door. The voices were low and intermittent. He opened the door.

It was dark in the living room. There were no lamps on and the only illumination was the television, which was muted. There was music playing but Vikram couldn't determine its source. At first, all Vikram could see, were bodies. Then he recognised Alasdair, slumped on the floor, his back propped against the sofa. He also noticed the girl from a few days ago, now fully dressed. She had her eyes closed and was slumped over another body. There were six people in total: three men, two women, and one unknown. Alasdair was holding a bucket. He turned to Vikram, his movements sluggish.

Alright Vikram. This is Vikram everyone. He's mi landlord.

Two of the others looked over at him. They nodded lazily as they processed the information. The air was pungently sweet and smoky. Vikram suddenly felt silly clutching his hot parcel of chips and he put them on the table.

What are you doing?

Alasdair stared at Vikram, as though he couldn't really comprehend his question. But then he nodded, Easy skanking.

Alasdair smiled as he said this. One of the girls laughed. Vikram noticed a piece of silver foil on the floor, blackened with heat and stained with a treacly residue.

What's the bucket for?

Alasdair smiled again, Got to have a bucket, ant yer, when you get scagged up.

The girl laughed again. Vikram left the room. He went into the kitchen and poured himself a large glass of wine. He'd left the chips in the living room. He made himself a ham sandwich and carried the glass and the plate up to the bedroom. He got into bed and put the television on. He ate the sandwich mechanically. He'd been looking forward to the chips. He drank the wine.

When Ruth came back from work, Alasdair and his friends had left. Vikram was relieved. She wanted to know why the living room was a mess and what the smell was. Vikram described the incident.

Smackheads in my home! I'm not having smackheads under my roof!

Vikram tried to calm her down. He said that Alasdair was just experimenting. He was young, it was only natural that he'd want to try things out, especially forbidden fruit.

Crap. He's a smackhead. And I want him out!

Vikram tried another tack. Perhaps he'd been mistaken. Perhaps they were just smoking dope. The room had been dark. He wouldn't like to condemn a man without knowing the full facts. Perhaps he could talk to Alasdair. A firm word.

Fat lot of good that will do!

Vikram had never seen Ruth so angry. Her face was contorted with hate, and her eyes were black with rage. She looked ugly and frightening. She reminded him of his mother, when he was a child. She would get that look, just before she beat him. It was the first time he had thought of her as being like his mother. The thought repulsed and disconcerted him. He put the thought to the back of his mind and tried to reason with her, but it was no use, she was in an absolute rage.

That night, when they went to bed, Vikram tried to cuddle up to Ruth, but she pushed him away.

Please, Ruth, don't. Let's not fall out over it.

He tried to hold her again, but she screamed at him and pulled the quilt tightly around her body. Vikram couldn't sleep. His heart was pounding in his chest, and he could feel a dull pressure building in his head. He got up and stood by the window. He looked out of a gap in the curtains. He looked at the orange street lights, and the lights from the houses. The lights were bleeding into each other. His eyes were watering. He was trembling with emotion.

He felt Ruth's arm slip round his waist. She gave him a squeeze, Come back to bed.

He didn't say anything. She gave him a squeeze again, I'm sorry.

They went back to bed. They fucked. Afterwards, bathing in their post-coital bliss, they agreed on a compromise. Vikram was to speak to Alasdair in the morning. He was to ensure that it never happened again. Ever. Vikram agreed to this. He promised.

Several weeks went by and the situation with the lodger got steadily worse. Vikram had spoken to Alasdair about his heroin use, and he'd promised Vikram he wouldn't do it again. Only now, the rent was overdue, and Alasdair was stalling him. Ruth had given Vikram an ultimatum, he either got the rent off Alasdair or he threw him out. Even if it meant physical removal. Even if it meant violence. Vikram had tried to assure her it wouldn't come to that.

But now it was two weeks overdue, and Ruth was not happy. They had argued three or four times about it already. Ruth had said she was not going to sort it out. It was up to Vikram. She was sick of sorting his mess out. And that was that. She had goaded him. What sort of a man was he? He was no sort of man at all if he couldn't even get a bit or rent money off a kid. He was pathetic. He was a miserable excuse for a man.

Vikram hadn't told Ruth, but he'd caught Alasdair taking heroin on two more occasions, both Wednesday nights when Ruth was on a late shift. On both occasions, Vikram had cleared up after Alasdair and his friends, and left the window open for a bit, to air the room. He'd made sure there was no evidence.

And now it was Wednesday again. Vikram was back in the Fighting Cock. He was on his fifth pint and he was wondering what to do. Dave and Barbara were still ignoring him. He wanted to ask them what was wrong but didn't have the courage. Perhaps he was being over-sensitive. But no, they weren't just ignoring him, they were visibly blanking him, making sure they made eye contact before turning away in disgust.

As he sat and pondered his predicament, a large, bearded man with a Staffordshire Bull Terrier came over to him. He stood over his table. He leant over to Vikram. The man's breath was hot and boozy.

You disgust me. You fucking junky.

The man sniffed, pulled at the dog lead and walked off. Vikram was in shock. What was all that about? He'd never taken drugs in his life, except for a few puffs of a spliff at a student party many years ago. It had made him feel nauseous and he'd never tried again. What was the man talking about? He must have mistaken him for someone else. But then it clicked. Alasdair must be a known drug user with a reputation. And people were adding two and two together and getting five. They were assuming that he was too. He looked around the pub. People were staring at him with wary or outwardly hostile eyes. He felt sick. He got up and left his beer on the table.

Outside he stumbled. He steadied himself using the wall by the side of the pub. He walked up the road. Ruth had given him his orders before she'd left for work. He was to get the money off Alasdair tonight, or forcibly remove him. If she came home and the problem hadn't been sorted out, she was going to leave him. Vikram laughed – surely she was joking. But her eyes were cold and hard – she was serious. How had it come to this?

When he got to the house, he could see the living room window and the faint illumination from the television. Alasdair was in there, with his druggy mates. What was Vikram to do? He couldn't kick him out now. What would his mates do? What if they turned nasty on him? He'd never argued with someone on drugs. What if they got violent? One of them might have a knife. It was best not to confront them. He turned around. He was walking but he didn't know where. The streets were desolate. He ended up at a bus shelter. He sat down on a plastic bench. It started to rain – fine, ineffectual drizzle.

It was cold. He pulled his collar up and put his hands in his pockets. Ruth would be back soon. She would find Alasdair. She would do her nut. She would pull her face the way his mother used to. Ruth and Vikram hadn't had sex now for nearly three weeks. They'd been together for five years, and throughout that time, they hadn't gone more than a day or two without sex.

It wasn't just Vikram, Ruth had always seemed to want it as much as he did.

Only now, neither of them seemed bothered. Vikram kept thinking of his mum every time he got into bed, and he just didn't feel like it. Ruth hadn't objected – she'd hardly touched him in all that time. Vikram watched his breath condense in front of his face. It was mesmerising and several minutes went by, without any thoughts, just his breath condensing like steam rising from the cooling towers that were the landscape of his childhood.

He was shivering now. He should talk to Ruth, that's what he should do. But somehow, he knew that wouldn't work. He just wanted to go home. He wanted his home back, the way it had been before Alasdair. Just him and Ruth. He would go back now and throw him out. But he didn't move. He slumped down on the bench and shivered.

a better devil

I've tried three times now. Last time was in April. You get spring fever. You think you can escape. I went to the Interchange. There's a train there goes to my sister's place. I just remember the voice from the tannoy. It was announcing the train times but then it went all weird. The announcer's voice rasped. It sounded like someone had slit his throat. And there were people. So many different types of people. Different races. Different sizes. Their mouths gaping open. The colours of their coats flashed. I could hear the colours jar. I could feel the lights above me pierce through my skull, like the crown of thorns through the head of Jesus Christ. I just remember collapsing onto the bag and sucking the straps. Biting hard into the plastic handles. Like dog's ears. I could hear the dog yelp and whimper as I bit hard into its sinew and muscle. I sprawled across the corpse of the dog, all wet with mud. It was warm and soft. The dead dog was warm and soft and it growled in a gentle way. It growled and snarled in order to comfort me. Two women were shaking me. You ok? Is there someone we can ring? And I just thought, don't ring him. Whatever you do. I don't want to go back there. I tried to stand up. There was no dog. Just my bag packed with a change of clothes and some make-up.

The two women were stood over me. Do you need an ambulance?

We can ring one for you if you like. I couldn't think straight. I couldn't think. The second time I tried it I ended up in Lynfield Mount. They gave me something really strong. Almost knocked me out. I just remember my mouth. It was really dry and I couldn't swallow. I was sitting in the community room. There was this man who thought he was blue and was from a planet where everything was blue. It should have been funny. It should have made me laugh. But it didn't. His hair was all stuck up and his eyes were on stalks. I could hear all this commotion in the reception room next door. It was him. I could hear him shouting. She's in there. I know it. You better get her or I'll get her myself. I could hear the nurses tell him he had to leave the building. Next thing he's running through the community room. He sees me and runs straight at me. Two male nurses behind him. Running. They grab him. Trying to restrain him. He's punching one of them in the face. Then the other. They fight back. I can't see what's happening. It's all too fast. Punching. Kicking. Howls. Bared teeth. One of the nurses has pulled his alarm. The bells are going off. Next thing there's another four male nurses. Takes six of them to hold him down. He's foaming at the mouth like a rabid dog. Next thing I know, it was five o'clock in the morning. I must have got out because there was snow on the ground. I didn't have any shoes or socks on, but I couldn't feel the cold. I couldn't feel my feet.

Come on, love, why don't you come with us. There's a café round the corner. A nice hot cup of tea. Or a milky coffee. They are helping me to my feet. One of them takes the bag. We go to the café. Sit in a corner. I drink a milky coffee with three sugars. We can't leave you like this, love. There must be someone we can call. Have you got a husband, maybe? Yeah, yeah, I'm married. What's he called? Have you got his number? The first time was no good. I didn't even get to the end of the street. I thought he was asleep. I was sure he was. I was still in my nightie under my coat. He was there before I even got to the bus stop. Put his arm around me and led me back home.

We couldn't leave you like that, could we? You see some folk now and they don't bother. There was a woman attacked on a train the other week. I read about it in one of them free newspapers. The train was full of commuters. No one batted an eyelid. But we're not like that. Come on, love, give us your husband's number and we'll ring him for you. It's not safe in a place like this, this time of night. There's all sorts round here. A fella got jumped a few days ago, by four lads. Kicked hell out of him. Left him for dead. All they stole was his phone.

Come on, let's get you home. I don't want to go home. I don't know where to go. I don't want to give them the phone number. But I give them his number and they ring him. He picks me up in his white van and takes me home again.

108

henry the hoover

I had no hoover. My old one broke. And I had no money. I used to use a dustpan and brush. But it was the hairs. Billy's hairs. Some terriers don't moult much but Billy leaves his hairs over every surface. I knew I should have got a patterned carpet. It was a mistake to get a plain colour. But I had a beige carpet and someone spilt red wine on it. My friend said, Pour white wine on it. I said, I've only got this. It was a bottle I was saving for Christmas. She said, Well, it's up to you – keep your wine or keep your carpet. So I poured half a bottle over the stain and soaked it up with a towel. It didn't work. I scrubbed and scrubbed. It was always there afterwards: a ghost of a stain. When I got a new carpet, I got a claret coloured one.

Five years I've had it and not a drop of wine spilt. I was getting down on my hands and knees twice a day, using a damp cloth, to pick up all the hairs. Then, one day, I was walking past the post office and I saw a sign in the window. It was only thirty quid and I just had enough. It was a good hoover. One of those Henry hoovers. A big fat red face on the front. All smiley and happy.

Here's the thing, when something has a face, you talk to it, don't you. It must be instinct because I've never talked to any other domestic device. I've never talked to the washing machine, or the kettle, for instance.

I sometimes stare at the kettle, at my reflection in the chrome surface, all distorted. But I've never spoken to it. I'd get Henry out of the cupboard. He wasn't easy to store. Wherever you put him he sort of spread out to fill the space. His arm always stuck out more than it needed to. I used to tell him off. There's no need to take up all this room, I'd say. Why can't you fold up nice and neat like the ironing board? But I'd plug him in and start working with him, and I'd say, I'm sorry I shouted at you. You're a hard worker and a good worker, you deserve to let your hair down once in a while.

He just smiled up at me. Such a lovely smile. I'd put him back in the cupboard. Now you be good for Mummy. No taking up all that space. Think about others. I'd close the door until the next day when I'd go and get Henry out again. He'd be all spread out once more, not caring about how much space he took up. I can take you back to where you came from, you know. I've still got the address. Think about it. I liked it there, if you really want to know. What? You heard. Well, that's just charming, isn't it. And what did she have that I've not got? A nice big cupboard with a big window, a lovely pair of curtains, and a personality. Right. That's it. If you think I'm going to hoover gently today, you've got another think coming. And I made a point. I slammed his mouth up against the skirting boards as hard as I could as I hoovered the carpet. I pressed his mouth hard into the dirt. Teach him a lesson. Now you be good for Mummy tomorrow, and I'll be nice to you, I said, as I locked him away.

I felt bad about it afterwards. You shouldn't lose your temper. If you do then you are as bad as them. You have to set an example. So the next day, I said, I'm sorry about treating you rough, I won't do it again. And I was extra careful with him. I even took out a soft cloth afterwards and gave him a bit of a polish. Lovely, I said. He was all shiny. Can I stay out for a bit? How do you mean? It gets stuffy in that cupboard. I can't breathe. Can I stay here with you and watch a bit of telly? I thought about it. No harm I supposed. I parked him up next to my armchair and turned on the Discovery channel. They have some good documentaries. We watched something about an Alaskan family that live in the wilderness. Then something about deep sea divers looking for a buried hoard of gold. This is nice, he said. Very civilised. I patted his head. Give my arm a scratch, he said. I took his arm in mine and gently scratched along the length. He made appreciative noises. I stroked around his mouth. He groaned.

Later that night, when I was switching off the telly and getting ready for bed, he said, I could sleep in your room if you like. I'm not sure, I said. I'm a light sleeper. I won't disturb you. I don't snore. You better not, I said. I took him in my arms, cradling him with his arm over my shoulder and carried him up the stairs. I put him down next to the bedside cabinet. You'll be alright there, I said, as I got undressed and climbed under the sheets. I stroked the top of his head and switched the light out.

Are you awake? It was dark, just a pale blue light from the phone charger. You've woke me up, I said, I was sleeping. It's cold, he said. Can I get under the covers? There's no room, I said. Go to sleep. I won't wriggle, he said. No, now go back to sleep.

I don't know how it happened but when I woke up the next morning, his arm was round me and his mouth was resting on my breast. You're going back in your cupboard, I said. I got dressed and carried him downstairs.

Things were never the same after that. I used to love that hoover. He got into every crack and crevice. He picked up every one of Billy's hairs. I used to love hoovering with Henry smiling at me. It made it easier. But after that, he wouldn't work as hard. I noticed him spitting out some of Billy's hairs. Then there was a bit of fluff in the hallway. I went over and over it with Henry, but he refused to pick it up. I told him. I warned him. But he just wouldn't do what I expected him to.

It was shortly after that, I left him too close to the fire. When I went to plug him in the next day, I got such a shock. All his face had melted. I tried to hoover with him, but I kept looking at his melted face. It was awful. I put him in the cupboard under the stairs. I can't stand to look at him anymore.

112

between the lights

1

The Man was driving through the west side of town when he saw The Girl. It was dark and the lights from his car formed piss-yellow eyes on the black road. The Man stared at the piss-yellow eyes and the piss-yellow eyes stared back. The Man imagined the piss-yellow eyes were the eyes of his boss. He could see the head of his boss form around the piss-yellow eyes: his bald head, his fat neck, his noose tie. The Man was driving a grey Mercedes with a scratch on the rear side. He was driving past boarded-up buildings. He was driving past a boarded-up archway where The Girl was standing.

The Man clocked The Girl but kept on driving. He was thinking about his day. It had been a bad day. Every day was a bad day now. He didn't want to think about his day. He thought about his desk. His desk was cool and clean. He had a large LCD monitor and a keyboard without any inscriptions. The keyboard featured individually weighted keys. He'd had it imported from Germany. Next to his keyboard was an A4 Moleskine ruled notebook and a silver Rotring Rapid PRO pencil. No ornaments or trinkets. He liked the items on his desk. They helped him to relax.

The Man did a U-turn at the end of the street and drove back on the other side, slowing down as he approached The Girl. He pulled up some distance away, killed the lights, then killed the engine. The Girl was wearing a black puffer jacket, loose fitting jeans, trainers and a navy blue Thinsulate hat. The Girl was standing in the doorway of a disused shop. The Girl had her hands in her pockets and was staring at the pavement. Even from this distance, The Man could see that beneath the street garb, chosen no doubt to deflect attention, her skin was fresh and smooth. The Man watched her for some time until The Girl shuffled up the street. Her breath condensed into a white cloud as she exhaled. The Man waited until The Girl had gone some way up the street towards Broken Road and then started his engine again.

2

The Girl was in an open-plan apartment. The Man she had only just met was showing her around. He was dressed in a grey suit with a white shirt and a grey tie. On his feet were brown brogues. They looked expensive but The Girl didn't know anything about shoes. She didn't know anything about suits. She didn't know anything about shirts. Her name was Maria, she was seventeen years old, and she was beginning to regret agreeing to come back to The Man's flat.

So, like I say, this is the pad. What do you think? The Man said. The Man was standing in the middle of a large room. He made a flourish with his arms. She noticed his gold watch. That was probably worth a few notes too. The room was mostly bare. There were plinths of different heights with sculptures on them and abstract oil paintings on the walls. The Girl thought that the room looked cold. The product of a dull mind. There was a large flat screen mounted on one wall and it reflected her silhouette and that of the man's. He wasn't much taller than her, although he was broader. Not muscular, just heavier. She wondered, if it came to it, whether he would be able to overpower her. She could always kick him in the bollocks. Nature's way of evening up the score. No matter how big the man, he always doubled up with a swift boot in the nuts. She'd seen men throw up, even pass out with the pain.

It's posh, she said.

The Man smiled. He seemed pleased with her response.

This is the main room. There's a great view of the city up here. Completely shut off.

The Man ushered her to the largest window. The Girl looked out over the buildings. The city was lit up with white and yellow light, but between the lights it was black.

I'm not saying everyone who lives here is a scumbag. Obviously, you're not a scumbag. I'm Steve by the way. Don't think I said my name. Anyway, like I say, it was funny bumping into you tonight. Well, maybe not funny, but you know what I mean. You're... you're alright, aren't you? I can take you to the hospital?

The Man moved close and tried to touch her where her face was cut and bruised. The Girl flinched. She moved away. The cut was stinging and the bruise throbbing.

I'm fine.

Right, ok then... It actually looks quite serious. I'd be happy to run you to A and E.

The Girl remembered the last time she had been in A and E. She remembered the blood. She remembered the pain. She remembered the police.

That's not... I'd rather you didn't. Thanks.

The thing is with head wounds – best to get them checked out.

He was probably right, but she didn't want to go anywhere near a hospital.

It's cold in here, she said at last. Even though it wasn't.

I'm the hot-blooded type. It's set at a constant of twenty-one degrees. I can override that if you like. Would you like that?

Yes.

He opened a white door which concealed a grey panel. He fiddled with the red buttons.

How about twenty-four degrees?

The Girl didn't answer. She was trying to remember what average room temperature was from her physics class in school. Her teacher was a perv. She'd heard about it from some year elevens. The Man finished adjusting the thermostat.

So, like I say, I'm Steve.

The Man offered her his hand to shake. The Girl looked at the gold watch again. It glimmered like a mirror. She looked at the clasp. It was one of those with a safety feature, so that you had to wrestle it off the wrist. Either that, or machete the fucker off. The Girl didn't take his hand, The Girl looked around the room instead. The Man waited for her to offer her name but The Girl didn't. The Girl walked over to the nearest plinth and picked up a vase. She didn't know what it was, but if she'd asked The Man he would have explained that it was late nineteenth century, Japanese. All she could see was that it was orange and gold and turquoise, with a complicated pattern that wrapped itself around the surface. The Man watched nervously as The Girl held it in her hands.

Right, well, we can do all the formalities later.

The Girl turned the vase over and looked at the base. She'd seen a man in a tweed jacket and a bow tie do this once on the television. The Man took the vase off her.

Better have that back. You've no idea what it's worth.

The Man put it back carefully, adjusting it so that it was in the same position it had been before. The Man explained that it was a rare item and he'd won it at an auction. It was hand painted with exquisitely fine detail. A rare example of its type.

Have you eaten? No, course not, I kind of interrupted you there. Sorry about that. How can you do that? I mean, it's wrong. You do know that, don't you? I don't want to get on my high horse or anything, but if you lose sight of, I mean... Well, anyway, I can cook you something. Would you like that? I'm a good cook. I watch all the programmes. Jamie Oliver, Gordon Ramsey.

The Girl had heard of Jamie Oliver. She used to watch telly when she lived at the hostel. And then before that at the home. But she didn't miss it now. It was a habit and once you'd broken a habit you were free. She walked to the next plinth and examined another vase. The Man hovered around her nervously. He had gone to an auction house in London for that vase. He had bid against three other men and one woman. He had paid more than he'd intended for that vase, but now it was his. The Girl liked watching The Man eye her nervously. It amused her.

Anyway, like I say, bit of a coincidence. I mean, I don't normally go out at night. I go out. I've got friends. Of course I have. But I don't go out, out...

The Man waited for his chance, then he took the vase off her and returned it to its precise spot. She watched as he turned the vase round so that it faced exactly the same way as it had before.

I just felt like a drive. Got a bit lost. You've got to be careful haven't you. *You* must have to be really careful. Especially. I would have thought. Anyway, sit down, make yourself at home. I'll make us a cup of tea, or would you prefer wine. I've got a bottle in the fridge.

The Girl craved alcohol.

Whatever.

I've been getting into the Italians recently. Or would you prefer a cup of tea? Or I've got coffee. You can have a coffee if you like. Would you like a coffee? It's a rainforest blend. It's really complex.

Vodka, whiskey, gin, brandy. The stronger the better, The Girl was thinking. Even a beer.

What are you having? she said.

Oh sod it. Let's crack open a bottle, shall we?

Do you live on your own?

Er... yes.

You're not married then?

No.

Or seeing anyone?

Er... no... Ok, wine it is then... take your coat off. Make yourself cosy.

The Man walked into the kitchen area. The Girl went back to the window and stared out across the dead city. The dead city was dead with dead people. The dead city was a crematorium stuffed with stiffs, rotting in boxes. It was like so many places she'd lived, only bigger and deader. More stiffs, more rotting boxes.

The Man returned with a bottle of white and two glasses. He put the glasses on the dining table. Then thought better of it and returned with two coasters. He unscrewed the top of the bottle. He filled both glasses halfway.

Good view or what? I wanted to be high up, you know, for the views. During the day it's different. It's light for starters. He laughed at his own joke. Obviously. But at night, it could be anywhere... Oh, here you go.

The Man handed the wine to The Girl. The Girl drank from the glass.

What do you think?

It tasted of nothing. But it was cold and it was booze.

It's nice.

Quite light but plenty of body. Lots of fruit. Can you taste apricot?

It tasted like chilled water. It tasted of thin air.

Is that what it is?

And orange blossom.

Right.

There was a bit of controversy about the aroma. Some tasters thought it was big and ripe, but others described it as a bit thin. I'm with the big and ripe camp... Please, take off your coat.

The Girl stared at The Man. She didn't take off her coat. She glugged the wine. Eventually it would numb the pain.

Are you still cold? I can turn the heating up again.

I'm fine.

Let me take your coat then.

The Girl took off her coat and hat. She put the hat in her coat pocket and handed her coat to The Man.

Now that's better. Isn't it? I'll hang it up.

The Man took her black puffer jacket in one hand as though he were handling a dead rat. He placed it on the floor of the laundry room and washed his hands. He dried them and returned.

There, that's much better. Now let's sit down. The cushions are really comfy. Or there's the chair if you prefer.

There was a large spherical chair made of transparent plastic. It was suspended from the ceiling by a chrome chain. There was a crimson cushion in the base. It looked like something out of an old sci-fi film, where the future was always clean and bright and plastic. It didn't look comfortable.

Which do you prefer? I remember as a kid there was one on this programme called Vegas. Long before your time. He was a private investigator called Dan Tanna. He had a chair just like this, and an open fire in the middle of the room. And a circular sofa. I've got the sofa on order. Size of a boat.

It was only then that The Girl noticed that there was no sofa. It didn't look, from the lack of furniture, that he was in the habit of entertaining guests. The Man laughed but The Girl was not impressed. The Man entered the kitchen area again. He returned with a recipe book.

Now then, there's a recipe in here for sea bass. I could do us sea bass stuffed with herbs. With a mushroom potato and a salsa verde? It's what Jamie cooked for Tony Blair at that summit a few years ago. Imagine that, cooking for Tony Blair.

He realised as he said this that she probably had no idea who Tony Blair was. It was a few years now since he had been in power, and besides, the young weren't interested in party politics. He wasn't really interested himself, come to think of it.

I've never had sea bass.

At least she didn't think she had. The only fish she'd eaten were covered in batter, and she'd never known exactly what sort of fish that was.

There you go then. First time for everything.

It would have to do, she supposed. She wasn't really keen on the fish she had eaten before, but she was so hungry she felt sick.

I'm very grateful, she said.

What for?

For what you did tonight.

Well. It was nothing really. I could see why he was angry, but he was completely out of order. It needed someone with authority to stand up to him. That's all it was.

Still.

Anyway, sea bass... or how about a bit of baked trout?

I've never had trout either.

Really? You've never lived in that case. I think we better play it safe. Go for the sea bass. If it's good enough for Tony, it's good enough for us.

The Man consulted his book. It had been a while since he'd cooked the dish and he wanted to re-familiarise himself with the process.

How long you been here? The Girl said.

The Man had only been there six months.

Oh, let me think. Getting on for ten years.

Then he wondered why he'd lied. It was silly. There was no need. Perhaps she would think he was less permanent though if he told her he had only just moved.

Alone?

You like to cut to the chase, don't you? We can chat later. Let's eat. It'll take me about half an hour. Just give me a shout if you want anything. Why don't you watch some telly. The dibber's on the table.

Without a sofa.

Eh?

You've lived here ten years. Alone. Without a sofa.

She was no fool, this girl. He was going to have to watch his back.

Three hundred channels, so you should find something you like. Right, I'll get cracking. Don't go away.

The Girl watched as The Man disappeared with his book under his arm.

I'll see what I can get from this cunt, The Girl thought.

3

The Girl and The Man were sitting at the table. The Girl was wearing The Man's dressing gown. She had a towel wrapped around her head. As she shovelled in the last of her meal, she noticed that her hunger pangs had gone. She no longer felt dizzy. She no longer felt sick. She felt clean and warm now the flat had heated up. They sat in silence and drank wine.

Like I say, I don't have a problem with it. Just wish you'd said.

Sorry. I wanted a bath.

I'm sure you did.

She had left a ring of filth around the white porcelain tub. She thought about wiping it off with a flannel but then decided not to bother. It wasn't her tub.

And you said make yourself at home.

I know I did.

So I did.

She had made herself at home. She had used his bubble bath. She had used his soap. She had used his shampoo. She had used his conditioner. She had used his razor and his shaving cream. She had used his moisturiser.

That's fine, like I say, it's not a problem. Just wished you'd mentioned it. Keeping sea bass warm is, er, problematic. Still, no harm done, eh? Tastes nice, doesn't it?

The Girl nodded. In fact, it was the best thing she'd tasted in her entire life. She realised that it wasn't fish she didn't like, it was the fish she had tried before that she didn't like. Greasy fish, battered fish, bland fish. She could still taste the herbs and the salsa verde. Her mouth was still watering.

I knew you'd like it.

It's okay.

It's really tasty, isn't it?

It's fine.

Great... Anyway, like I was saying. No funny business. I'll sleep on the floor. On the cushions. You can have my room. I'll change the bedding for you. Not that it's dirty, but you know.

The Girl ignored The Man. She helped herself to the wine.

Oh sorry. Nice, isn't it?

The Girl drained the bottle. The Man looked at his empty glass.

Tell you what, I'll open another.

The Man went to the fridge. He opened it and took out another bottle.

You can have the rest of that if you like. I'll make a start on this.

He came back with the bottle and filled his glass. He sat back down at the table.

What were you doing?

The Man fiddled with his glass. He held it by its stem. He twisted it around. He swilled the liquid. He took a sip of the wine and placed it back on the table.

How do you mean?

Well, you weren't walking your dog, were you?

I don't have a dog.

That's what I'm saying.

I was just out for a drive. Sometimes I like to do that. I like to go for a drive. Helps me relax.

Were you dogging?

The Man choked on his wine. His face was flushed with blood. He picked up a napkin and wiped his mouth.

I'm sorry?

You must have been dogging.

I don't know what you mean.

Of course you do.

The Girl had been given the tip-off from a dosser she knew. Once a month the doggers met in the car park behind the old fish market on Broken Road. They would bring food and drink: picnics, flasks of hot coffee and soup; beer, wine and spirits. Sometimes they would wear animal masks: foxes, badgers, pigs. It meant that their sight was restricted behind their plastic shields. She had tried her luck before and hit rich. A bottle of Smirnoff Ice, a packet of wine gums and a bag of pork pies. They were too distracted with the floor show to pay her mind. But not this time.

Would... would you like a pudding? The Man said.

The Girl didn't respond. She was thinking that The Man was a pudding. That he looked like a pudding. He was wearing the uniform of the office drone: an ash-coloured suit, white shirt and plain tie. But his face had a bloated aspect. His skin was soft and shiny – over-moisturised.

I've got some good puddings.

She thought back to her childhood. At one of her foster homes they'd had pudding and chips every Friday as a treat from the chip shop. There were suet puddings with steak and kidney filling. They looked like the head of a baby, soft and shiny. You could dip your spoon in and scoop out the insides. His skin had the same pallor as suet. The same waxy sheen.

Well, just say if you do.

She had never trusted men in suits. Wolves in sheep's clothing. What were they hiding? Why did they want a noose around their necks? Or was it meant to be an arrow pointing to their dicks? Hey girls, come and get some, it's all yours.

I'm full, thanks.

Tell you what, let's just crash for a bit.

The Man stood up and went over to the spherical chair. But then he stopped. He had changed his mind.

You can have the chair. I'll have the cushions.

The Man sat on the cushions on the floor. He watched as The Girl approached the chair and eased her way in. It swung back as she did and she steadied it with her bare feet.

So are you a boss then?

Er, yes, sort of. I'm a senior exec.

Do you tell people what to do?

Well, it's a little complicated.

How do you mean?

The company is making a few changes. I'm sort of... I used to have my own team but we're shuffling things around at the moment. It's a bit hard to explain.

So you don't tell people what to do?

The Man shifted his position. He looked uncomfortable. He leaned back on one elbow but then sat forward again. He crossed his legs and put his arms across his thighs.

Do you like that chair then? he said.

The Girl liked the chair. It was more comfortable than it looked. She gave a non-committal nod.

Good... You can sit on it all night if you like. I'm happy 'on the floor'. More than happy... Really.

He shifted uncomfortably again.

Do you have a secretary and an office and a phone and all that?

Like I say, there's a lot of restructuring going on. I won't really be in the picture until the dust settles. We're trying a new system.

He talked a lot of shit, this man. But she didn't mind. He was easy to talk to. She felt that she could trust him despite the suit. Perhaps he was an exception. He certainly didn't strike her as dangerous. He was the sensitive type – in touch with his feelings. Considerate of others, especially women. In other words, he was a push over. She had landed on her feet.

How do you mean?

Well, we're moving from a closed office environment to an open one.

What's that then?

It's where you get rid of things like offices and everyone works in a big open space.

It's supposed to be more creative.

It sounded like a bag of bollocks. But she'd never worked in an office. She'd worked on the streets. She'd worked in a shop. When she was a kid, she'd worked for an elderly woman at the bottom of the street. She'd done her shopping for her, made her fire by twisting old newspaper, mowed her lawn.

And is it?

Early days... Would you like some more wine?

The Girl nodded. The Man got up and drained the bottle into both their glasses.

So, you've still not told me about you.

Not much to tell.

I mean, you don't have to... You can if you like, but don't feel that there's any pressure to do so... I'll carry on talking about me if you want.

She didn't really mind. Although he had nothing to say, his voice was low and soft, and she preferred listening to others to doing the talking herself. There was always the danger when you talked that you'd say something.

I think it's very therapeutic. The talking cure. I always feel so much better after a good chat... My dad was a very quiet man. Keeping it all inside. And I saw that... As a kid... Even then I knew, you know, that it was unhealthy.

Where is he now?

Er, actually he's in a hospital. Well, it's not so much a hospital, it's more like a hotel. There's a menu and a piano, and fresh flowers, and everything. Only, with nurses instead of bellboys. Costs me a fortune. He's getting better.

What's wrong with him?

Well, it's not that there's anything wrong with him. I mean, if you met him, you'd probably like him. He's a sweet guy really. Only, he's, what you call, officially at least, clinically depressed. They call them clients, not patients, so you see, it's more of a service they offer.

So he's a nutter. Is that what you're saying?

Well, no, I mean, I wouldn't say that, I wouldn't use that terminology. I'd make the comparison that it's like having toothache. You go to the dentist and he pulls it out. Or *she* pulls it out – could be a female dentist. Let's not be genderist... anyway, the point is, end of toothache. Do you see what I mean? It's a bit like that, only it's in his head. The problem is. Not that you'd want someone to pull it out. Well, not literally.

The Girl knew about nutters. she'd had plenty of experience. Harmless nutters, ones that gave you the creeps, ones that pissed themselves, ones that cried like babies, ones that refused to talk or go out of their rooms. Nutters who thought the world was out to get them. Nutters who wanted to get you.

But if you have toothache, that doesn't necessarily make you a nutcase, she said.

Well, no, I don't suppose it does. It's just that... well, ok, I concede to your point, on one level you could say, that, yes, he's a nutcase.

Right.

Anyway, this is nice. This is very nice. Good wine, good company... I've made up your bed. While you were in the bath. Fresh sheets.

My bed?

Well, my bed, technically, but for tonight, we can call it your bed, if you like. Would you like that?

Maybe I should go.

Go where? I mean it's late. The hostels will be closed. Where will you stay?

She could always find a doorway or an abandoned building. She had slept on the floors of old mills, old shops, old factories. She had broken into empty houses and slept there. Once she slept in the cellar of a church building. It was damp and smelled of rat shit. Another time she broke into a canteen on the roof of a car garage. She'd found some porn mags and a box of dominos.

Well, that's settled then. So any time you want to get your head down, just say.

I will.

Don't think it's rude.

I won't.

It's just that I can't go to sleep until you do. If you see what I mean.

I see.

She enjoyed watching him squirm.

I like to get an early night during the week. It's the job – it's very high pressured. Got to re-charge those batteries.

He waited for a response. She didn't give one. She drank some more wine.

Would you like some music?

I don't mind.

I'll put some on, shall I... What sort of thing do you like?

I'm easy.

Right.

He went over to the hi-fi and started to fiddle with it. It was a great system. It hadn't been on the market long. It had its own hard drive. Every time he put a CD in, it automatically ripped it. Eight hundred gig of memory too, so it could hold thousands of discs. He spent three months ripping discs. Most of it was available on Spotify, but he didn't like the compression rates. This way there was no compression of the music files. He searched through the menus looking for something suitable. He found just the right thing.

I think you'll like this, he said. It's quite chilled out, but a bit quirky. See what you think.

The music started and he watched The Girl for a reaction. He hoped she enjoyed Enya as much as he did.

What do you think?

It was slow, quiet. There wasn't much of a beat. It sounded boring.

It's too early to tell.

Let me give you a push. It's nice to have a swing.

He walked over to the chair and stood behind it. He placed his hands close to where her buttocks were and gave it a push. The Girl started to swing.

This is nice... Actually, that wine's gone straight to my head. I feel quite stoned.

How do you feel?

Ok.

He leaned into the chair so that his groin was almost touching the clear plastic dome. He felt the warmth of her body and pushed again. He watched her swing. He lay back down on the cushions and propped his head up. She was swinging herself now with one leg on the wooden floor. As the swinging increased, her robe fell open a little and exposed a bare shoulder. The skin was pale and smooth. The Man felt guilty watching The Girl but he couldn't take his eyes off her.

I forgot to say. Your clothes are in the machine. It washes and dries. They should be ready now.

The Girl continued to swing. Her robe slipped a little further down her body. He tried not to show his enthusiasm. He watched her, mesmerised.

This reminds me of an episode of Vegas. Dan Tanna's house was in the desert. He used to drive his car into the front room. He had a remote control on his dashboard, so that the garage door opened as he drove up the driveway. He'd pull up by the side of the breakfast bar. He had a chair just like that, and this open fire in the middle of the room. He'd brought this woman back. He was fixing them cocktails at the breakfast bar. The music. The Girl was swinging. He came back into the room, and well...

Dan Tanna had gone over to the woman and kissed her. They'd ended up in bed together. But he didn't want to tell The Girl that. Instead, he said, Actually, I'm quite tired. He yawned to emphasise the point. Got to be up early in the morning. Got a big client.

He wished she would cover her shoulder up. At the same time, he was glad she hadn't. Was she aware that it had slipped down? Should he tell her?

It's a big contract. Virgin Trains. I thought the whole thing up myself. My boss loves it. We're going to get Mariella Frostrup to do the voice over.

Her voice. It's so...

He thought about Dan Tanna again. Only this time he was in bed with a different woman. It was Mariella Frostrup. The Girl was swinging harder. Her robe had loosened some more. He put his head back and as she swung over his prostrate body, he opened his mouth. He thought about Dan Tanna once more. Now he was in bed with The Girl. They were both naked and he was putting it in her over and over again.

4

That night The Man slept on the floor on the cushions and The Girl slept in The Man's bed. She took a chair and wedged it behind the door so that the handle of the door was wedged shut. She had a look round his room. There was a large walk-in wardrobe with ten business suits and ten formal shirts hanging up. There was a separate area for his ties. Another area for his socks and pants and a shelf for his shoes. What a geek, she thought. What a wanker.

Almost everything was white, except for those things that were grey. There was a chest of drawers. Inside the first drawer were a row of boxes. She opened the boxes one by one. Inside each one was a different pair of cuff links. What a sad twat, she thought. In the drawer below was a tracksuit. That made her laugh. She couldn't see him in a tracksuit. Perhaps he ran in his spare time or just liked to wear it round the house. She tried to picture him running in a tracksuit, or working out at the gym, but she couldn't. He was a sheep in a suit.

Finally, when she had checked every receptacle and every compartment of every receptacle, she climbed into his bed and felt the pillow's crisp coolness on her cheek. The bed was soft and the sheets were clean. It was a king size bed and she stretched out, enjoying the luxury and comfort of it. It had been a while since she had slept in a bed. She had never slept in a bed this luxurious. She lay back and closed her eyes. The day's events re-wound in her head. Then she thought about her own bedroom. The bedroom of her early childhood. The icicles on the window. The shadow of the chimney from the factory over the road. Her room was in constant shadow. It cast her in perpetual darkness. It loomed over her life. How she had wanted to climb that chimney to get to the light. She saw it reach up into the sky, a black silhouette, like an exclamation mark. Then she felt tired and quickly drifted into a deep sleep.

The Man woke up on the floor. The light from the window poured into the room. He didn't need blinds or curtains this high up. He wasn't looked on. He was above everything else. It took a few seconds for him to remember where he was. The room from this angle was unfamiliar. But then it came back to him. Last night and The Girl. His back ached but he smiled as he remembered The Girl's enjoyment of the food he had cooked. He pictured her swinging in the chair. He pictured her robe slipping down. He felt himself stiffen and he got up and showered.

He went to his bedroom to put on fresh clothes but something was stopping the door from opening. He tried again but it was wedged shut. She must have put something up against the door. He felt angry at first but then reasoned with himself. She was just a girl. He was a strange man – to her. She couldn't be blamed for taking this precaution. He knocked gently to wake her and waited. Nothing. He knocked a little louder. No response. He knocked even louder still but it was no good. He could not wake her.

He went to the dirty linen box where he'd thrown his shirt and underwear. He noticed something scruffy on the floor and he picked it up with thumb and forefinger. It was a doll. A dirty, dishevelled rag doll. It looked handmade. It was about four inches in height with a mucky white face: two cross stitches for eyes, a black stitched mouth. It wore a besmirched red pinafore dress, black tights, grey-white blouse. Its hair was gathered into pigtails. It repulsed him. He threw it in the bin and washed his hands in the sink.

He went back to the dirty linen box and took out his shirt and underwear. He sniffed. It didn't smell, but still it disgusted him to think that they had already been worn. He went into the bathroom, filled the sink with warm water and soap and washed them by hand. Then he took them to the dryer, placed them in the drum, and switched it on. It wasn't ideal, but it would have to do.

It was a fast machine. It wouldn't take long. Just time for a shave and a shower.

He got dressed in the still warm underwear and shirt and put his suit and shoes on. He was fastening his tie when the bedroom door opened and The Girl appeared. She was dressed in the same drab outfit she'd worn when he'd picked her up. She must have got up earlier and retrieved it from the dryer.

Oh, you're up. I didn't wake you, did I?

No.

Did you sleep well?

Yes.

Good.

Did you?

Not bad, thanks.

He wasn't used to sleeping on the floor. It was hard and he ached all over. His neck was stiff.

I'll get off then.

He was gripped with panic.

You're not going, are you?

The Girl shrugged, Well, I can't stay here, can I.

Er, well, actually you can. If you want that is.

I best not.

I'd love you to... I, I really enjoyed last night. It was lovely. I can cook for you again tonight if you like. I like having you around.

What for?

Just, well, the company really. It's a bit quiet up here at night. Not a lot going on. Gets a bit lonely to be honest.

How do you know I won't just walk off with all your stuff?

I don't.

I might do.

He weighed this up for a moment. You'd never get past security. The guy on the door knows everyone who lives here. In any case – you need one of these.

He took out a plastic card. It was a key pass. He showed it to her.

You can't get in or out without this.

He put the pass back in his wallet.

So I'd be trapped here, that's what you're saying.

Well, temporarily, yes... Tell you what I'll do, I'll go and see the concierge on my way out. I'll tell him you're my girlfriend—

Girlfriend?

No, you're right. Not girlfriend. Sister. I'll say you're my sister and that you're staying for a bit. They can issue me with a spare. Only takes twenty-four hours... You can watch TV. I've got DVDs, I've got books. Whatever you like really. Like I say, it would only be for today. There's eggs and milk in the fridge if you want breakfast.

He searched around for his briefcase. He picked it up and dusted it down even though there was no dust on it.

So what do you think?

I'm not sure.

It's up to you. But if I were you and it was a choice between a luxury apartment and the gutter, I know what I'd choose.

Right.

So are you staying or going?

I think it's best if I go. But thanks for the meal. And the bed. And you know, helping me out and all that. That bloke was nuts. He could have killed me.

Well, it's up to you, Maria, but I really don't think it's a good idea. Just stay another night. You've had a very nasty shock. Sometimes there's a delayed reaction. You should rest up until you've fully recovered.

It sounded odd him calling her Maria. But it was the made-up name she had given him.

I don't know, she said.

Please. Just one more night. It's great having you here. Makes the place sort of cosier somehow. Just for tonight.

Well, maybe just one more night then.

Great, so you'll stay then..? Great. I'll let the concierge know.

No need for that. I won't be needing a key. I'll get off in the morning.

Shit, shit, shit.

Fine. It's your decision.

He picked up his car keys, I'll be back about six.

He went out of the door. She waited for him to leave and then she started to search the apartment. She opened drawers and cupboards. The first drawer was filled with phone chargers, batteries and an assortment of tangled leads. The next contained napkins. Who has napkins? she thought. The cupboards were full of glassware and crockery, silver cutlery. Some of it looked valuable but she wasn't looking to steal anything. She could do that later, once she'd found it.

5

The Man swiped the key and entered his apartment. He whistled a tune as he heaved the shopping bags over to the dining table. He had managed to take a long lunch break and had gone into town to buy a few things for The Girl. He couldn't wait to see what her reaction would be. He looked around but there was no sign. He shouted her name. Nothing. He went into his bedroom. The bed wasn't made, but that didn't matter. He shouted again. Still no response. She couldn't have got out, could she? Not without a key. She couldn't have climbed out of the windows, they were too high up. Perhaps she had rang down to reception, and said she had been locked in by mistake. That would be easy to do. He hadn't thought about that this morning. His brain was never at its best at that time. Coffee, that's what it needed before it would spring into action. Then he heard the toilet flush and a moment later the door opened. There she was.

Were you shouting?

Sorry, didn't know where you were... How have you been?

Ok.

Great... Did you watch anything interesting?

One or two things.

Fantastic. How did you get on with the DVDs?

I didn't.

Not to worry. You can save them for another time... probably not your scene. A lot of foreign films... not that you wouldn't like foreign films, I'm sure you would, but they're not to everyone's taste.

Are they the ones in the locked cabinet?

The locked cabinet?

You've got two cabinets. One is locked.

It was probably stashed with porn. Lesbians in school uniforms, or buxom milkmaids in haylofts.

Oh, is it? I hadn't realised... So what did you do then?

Not much.

I hope you don't mind, but I've been doing a bit of shopping. I bought you a dress... Here, have a look.

He went over to the bags on the table and took out a red dress. He handed it to her with the label hanging out. Versace.

There you go. What do you think?

It's hard to say.

Oh, I got you some shoes too.

He went over to the bags again and pulled out a shoe box with the word, Givenchy on the top. He took off the lid, took out the shoes and handed them to her.

Try them on.

Later.

Please, put them on now. I'll avert my eyes.

The Girl was laughing inside. How easy it was to play these fools. A red dress, for fuck's sake. He was probably a Chris de Burgh fan.

The man turned away. The Girl left the room. The Man stood with his hands over his eyes. But then it dawned on him that she had left the room and he removed his hands from his eyes and put them in his pockets. He stood and waited. When she returned, she was wearing the dress and the shoes.

Wow! You look... really... what a transformation... what do you think?

It's ok.

She had been surprised that both the dress and the shoes were a perfect fit. He had obviously noted her size last night when he washed her clothes.

I knew you'd like it.

She just stood there, rather awkwardly. She fiddled with the hem of the dress.

Oh, I've got something else.

He reached into his pocket and took out an envelope.

Two tickets for the theatre tonight. An Alan Ayckbourn. Do you like Alan Ayckbourn?

Who?

He's written load of plays. They're very funny. You'll enjoy it. I was going to cook us something, but there isn't time now. But there's a good restaurant near the theatre. I thought we could eat out. What do you think?

Ok.

Right, just let me get out of my work clothes. And then, Alan Ayckborn here we come. It's been quite a day I'll tell you. Tell you what, should we have a quick glass first?

Ok. If you think there's time.

He went to the kitchen area and poured them both a drink.

What a bloody day, I'll tell you...If Mark Simpson died tomorrow, I have to confess, I would feel great relief. Funny thing is, when I first met him I actually quite liked him. He was charming, clever, confident. But then I learnt behind the confidence was arrogance and, actually, the thing is, a monstrous ego.

The Girl stood waiting for her glass.

He values himself too highly and what's more, he's bluffing about his achievements. I would like him to disappear, but first I would like him to suffer pain... Fern Britton. Bloody Fern Britton. Can you believe it?

My wine?

He said Mariella Frostrup found the advert tasteless. Can you believe that?! They offered us Lorraine Kelly, but I said I'd resign if we went with Lorraine Kelly. And I meant it.

The Girl went over to him and took the glass from his hand.

Oh, sorry, there you go. On top of that the computers decided to crash right in the middle of an important job.

Is he your boss?

Who?

Mark Simpson.

No, God, the thought of it. He's my Moriarty.

There's something I want to ask you about.

What's that?

My doll.

Your what?

My doll. I had a doll. It was in my pocket. You washed my clothes. Now it's gone. I've searched all over. I can't find it. Where is it?

Oh, that doll.

Where is it?

Well, I'll be honest. I thought it was a bit of rubbish.

You thought what?

It was dirty, and well, tatty.

What have you done with it?

I, er, disposed of it.

You did what?

I... I didn't think you'd want it. I put it in the bin.

Well, you better get it out again.

Well the thing is, he looked at his watch, the bins will have been emptied now. So I can't get it back.

You bastard.

Look, I'm sorry, I really am. I didn't mean to... I mean I didn't know it meant so much to you.

She walked up close to him so that she could see the holes in his skin.

You bastard.

She slapped him very hard across his face. He shouted out in pain and held his hand to his cheek.

I want my doll back.

I'm sorry.

Fucking sorry's no fucking good.

I don't deserve you, he said, then looking down at his feet said, I threw it away on purpose.

You bastard.

It disgusted me.

You—

It repulsed me.

The Girl slapped him again, only this time much harder. She almost knocked him sideways. The Man winced in pain. She slapped him once more and he winced and screamed out. He quivered with excitement.

I'm not staying here any longer. I'm going.

But you can't.

The Girl went to the door. She tried to open it but it was locked.

You need this, The Man said, and he took out the pass card. The Girl went to grab it off The Man but he put it back in his pocket just in time.

Stop messing about. Open the door.

I really didn't want to do this.

What are you talking about?

I can't let you leave I'm afraid.

Don't be stupid, Steve. Give me the key.

I'm afraid that's not an option. Don't leave me. Stay here. You can be my queen.

She went to get the key again. She lunged for his pocket. He knocked her back and she banged into the side of the table. The Givenchy bag fell to the floor. She lunged at him again. He grabbed hold of her but she had him by the hair. Then she had him by the throat. She was choking him. His face was turning red and his eyes were bulging. But then he launched a clenched fist to the side of her head and knocked her off her spot. He punched her in the face. He punched her in the face. He punched her in the face. She staggered. He punched her in the face. She fell to the floor. Unconscious.

6

When The Girl came round she was tied to a dining chair with Sellotape. She tried to shout out but she had been gagged. She was immediately aware of a dull throbbing pain around her eye and a sharper pain around her nose. She could see the tip of it, encrusted with blood. She looked around the room. The Man was swigging from a bottle of red wine. He had spilled some of it down his white shirt. He had taken off his tie and several buttons were missing, exposing his waxy flesh. He was sitting on the floor, weeping.

She watched his tears fall to the floor. She saw now that some of the stains on his shirt were blood stains. He looked over to her and saw her staring at him. He put the bottle down and dried his eyes.

I'm sorry. I'm so sorry. It's not like me... I mean, I've never done anything like this before. I just... I just couldn't stand the thought of it. Of losing you. I mean we've only just got to know each other and... and I think we stand a chance. I don't know. There are so few people in the world who...

He stared at her and began to weep again. He took a slug from the bottle.

Ok. Let's try again. I'm going to take off the gag. Promise me you won't scream this time. Promise me.

The Girl nodded. The Man removed the gag. The Girl screamed. The Man replaced the gag.

How can I trust you, Maria? I don't want this... do you think I want this? You tied up and gagged... it's the last thing I want. I just want to talk to you. I just want to know about you. Please. Let's just talk and be friends... we can start again. Pretend this never happened. Ok? Or we can just sit here with you gagged and tied to a chair. I don't want that, you don't want that. Please, let's give it another go shall we?

The Girl looked him in the eye and nodded.

Ok. I'm going to remove the gag. If you scream I'll put it back. Do you understand?

She nodded again.

Right, ok, let's try it once more.

The Man very hesitantly removed the gag.

There, that's better. Are you ok?

No, I'm not. I'm in pain. You fucking dick.

I really am sorry, Maria. I don't know what came over me. I'm not that sort of man. I've never hit a girl in my life before. I promise. It's so unlike me.

Get me some pain killers.

I've got Ibuprofen. I've got codeine. Which one?

Whatever's strongest.

I'll get you the codeine.

The Man went to the kitchen and took out a box. Inside was a blister pack of pills. He took two and put the packet back. Then he opened the cupboard again and took out two more and brought them over to The Girl.

Do you want some water?

Give me some of that wine.

Of course.

No, I'll have some of that whiskey over there.

She nodded to a whiskey box on the shelf behind the table.

The Bladnoch?

I don't give a fuck what it is.

But that's the only whiskey I've got.

It'll do.

It'll do? It's a thirty-year-old single malt. It's a collector's item.

Just give me a glass of it, you whining prick.

Ok, alright, hang on.

The Man had been saving the bottle. There was a webpage where you could watch its value appreciate. There was a graph of rare whiskies. The distillery had closed a few years ago and it was a good buy. It was a single malt of some vintage. He would have preferred to fill her glass with his own blood, but he uncorked the bottle and poured the whiskey into a tumbler.

Take this tape off.

But...

He saw that he would have to remove the tape for her to be able to grip the glass.

Take it off.

Ok, but only if you promise—

Just do it.

The Man went to un-tape her. But then changed his mind.

Ok then, but I'm only freeing the one hand.

The Man took some scissors and cut free one hand. He gave her the glass. He put the pills in her mouth. The Girl necked the whiskey.

What do you think?

What?

Of the whiskey?

It's whiskey.

Some of the tasters said that they could taste roasted coffee beans in it. And peach and cinnamon. He could taste the peach and the cinnamon but not the roasted coffee beans. He'd tried several batches but to no avail. The fruit had surprised him. Before his preference had been for peaty whiskeys but now his preference was for fruity whiskeys. And it was all down to the Bladnoch. And this was the last bottle he had.

Take this fucking tape off. I mean what sort of kidnapper are you? Haven't you ever heard of rope?

I don't have any. Sellotape's all I've got.

Take it off.

I can't do that, Maria. Not yet. I want to. Really I do, but I can't.

Why not?

I can't trust you yet. You've lost my trust. You need to gain it back. I just want to talk to you. If I untie you now, what's to stop you running off? What's to stop you going to the police?

I won't run off. Ok. I won't go to the police.

I wish I could believe you. I really do.

Look. I can't run to the police. Right. Does that make you feel any better?

What do you mean you can't run to the police?

I just can't. They'll arrest me.

What for?

It's a long story.

So tell me.

Why should I?

Because if I believe you, I'll untie you.

Will you?

I promise.

He hadn't decided yet what he was going to do with her. Untying her was one of his options.

I promise.

She didn't trust him. But what choice did she have?

It started way back.

What with?

I was put into care. A children's home. Then I was fostered out. Then I was put into care again.

What for? I mean, why were you put in care?

My mum. She was killed. When I was four.

How?

You might not remember it. It wasn't that big a story. He was called David Banks. He killed this woman, then he killed my mum. I think he was a bit disappointed.

What do you mean?

He wanted to be a serial killer. Only he got caught after two. You're not really a serial killer after two are you?

Suppose not.

I mean three's the minimum number, right?

Er, well, yes. I suppose so.

It got into the papers. It got mentioned in the news, but it wasn't a big story.

So what happened?

My dad didn't cope very well. I mean I don't think things were good before, but it didn't exactly help. He's Irish, bit of a pikey.

How do you mean?

A gypo right. Was brought up in a caravan. His mum used to make pegs, read palms, all that shit.

Really? Did you live in a caravan?

Nah! That all changed when he met my mum. He worked as a labourer. Building sites. Ground work. We had a council flat.

Right. Tough work I'd imagine.

When she died, he didn't cope so well. Took to the drink. Got laid off. Sort of fell apart. We got taken away.

We?

Me and my sister.

You've got a sister?

Yeah.

Younger or older?

Older. Two years.

Where is she now?

Fuck knows.

The Girl really didn't know where she was. Nor did she give a shit.

Was she a prostitute?

Who?

Your mum. Sorry. That was rude of me. It's just they normally are. I didn't mean anything by it.

No she wasn't, right. That's what fucks me off. That's what the papers said. She wasn't a fucking prostitute – you got that?

Ok. I'm sorry... I'm sorry.

She was just having a night out. Ok.

Ok, I'm sorry. Go on.

I slept in one bed with my older sister. She was shaking me. I didn't want to wake up, but she said that Mum wasn't home. It was nearly morning. We waited by the bus stop. But she wasn't on the bus.

So what happened?

A policeman told us she wasn't coming back. He told us that she was with God. We waited for her to come back from seeing God.

But she didn't.

Of course not, you prick. We were sent to a home. One day a man came to see us. They told us that the man was our dad. But I hardly recognised him. He drove us to his new house and we all lived happily ever after.

Right.

He let this sink in. He wasn't used to being played with like this.

But you didn't, right?

We did. It was lovely.

Come on.

He waited for her to respond. She stared at the floor. Still staring at the floor, she said, we got taken into care again a few months later.

Why?

Punishment. His punishment.

Where is he now?

Don't know. Dead, with any luck... I found out later that the bus stop where we waited, she was there.

Your mum?

Her dead body was in the grass verge by the side. We were four or five feet away from mum. Her arms were bound with cable ties. She'd been suffocated with a carrier bag and masking tape. That's how they knew it was him.

Fucking hell. I'm so sorry.

What for? It wasn't your fault. Was it?

How do you mean?

You're a man. So it's your fault.

He certainly seemed to like tying up women and gagging them in any case.

I'll be honest, I do sometimes feel guilty when I hear about stuff like that. That's why I feel so bad about... I couldn't watch *The Accused*. I had to walk out of the cinema, five minutes into the film... I thought, I'm a man, that's what men do. I must be bad. But then I think, I'm not like that. Not all men are like that. Some of us are ok.

She looked at her tied arm. And you're one of the ok ones?

Yes.

She waited for the bitter irony of this to sink in. She waited some more. It didn't sink in.

You saved me from that man—

Anyone would do that.

You brought me here. You've fed me, clothed me... Now you've got me tied to a chair. You must want something.

I don't.

You don't want anything?

I'm not a bad man.

I'm not sure that would stand up in court. Give me some more whiskey.

He poured another dram. She necked it in one. He poured again.

You didn't finish your story.

What?

Why you can't go to the police. I don't get it.

Like I say, it's a long story.

Go on.

We got fostered. We got split up. I got into trouble. Stealing. I ended back in care. Then when you're sixteen the state no longer has to look after you. They kick you out.

That doesn't seem fair.

No shit.

I mean that's just wrong.

She looked at him. A smart job, a smart suit, a luxury apartment.

You haven't got a fucking clue.

No. I can see that.

Anyway, I just sort of drifted. Got into trouble. Nothing much. Stealing mostly. Shoplifting. I had a flat. I was top of the list of vulnerable people. A homeless girl aged sixteen. They got me a place pretty quick. It was alright. I even got some work. In a shop. My social worker. Ruth she was called. She did everything she could. But it wasn't enough.

How do you mean?

I was drinking and all the rest of it, you know, having a proper good time. Parties, late nights. It all costs... I wasn't earning enough. Sort of drifted into stealing again. First it was the till at work until the owner copped me. Got the sack. Sort of went on from there. There was a bloke on the estate. He'd give me a shopping list. Things people wanted. This went on for months. I wasn't the only one. He had a group of us working for him. Bit of a modern-day Fagin. The thing is right, it was fun. It was a laugh. Sometimes they'd run after you. The shop workers. They never caught you though. You'd be buzzing for ages. Going over and over it with yer mates, picturing their faces in yer head and just screaming with laughter... Then the police set him up. We all got busted. I had a pretty bad record at that point. I was due in court. Ruth, my social worker, she said that I'd probably get a custodial sentence. I'd had a few cautions, a few fines, community service, suspended sentence. It was bound to be a custodial right?

So what happened?

I got my date in court. Only I didn't show up.

You didn't show up?

I fucked off out of the flat. I was sixteen and on the run. Been on the run ever since. They'll throw the book at me if they ever catch me. That was over a year ago... So you see, I can't go to the police, so you've got me right where you want me. Now what are you going to do?

She waited for him to respond but he said nothing.

You better tell me or I'm going to start screaming again.

Really. I don't want to do anything. I just want us to be friends. I know I've not exactly gone about it in the right way, but...

But what?

But that's what I want.

So untie me.

Do you promise not to run out on me?

I'm not promising you anything. Now untie me, you tit.

He thought about it again. Her story was plausible. There had to be a good reason why a young girl would be living on the streets. And this was as good a reason as any.

Ok, I'm going to untie you. Right. I trust you. You can stay here. I won't do anything. I don't want anything from you.

He reached across and untied her. He snipped the Sellotape. The Girl stood up and stretched her limbs. She winced in pain. She had pins and needles in her forearms. She could feel it pepper like nettle stings. She was aching all over. She looked at The Man and shook her head, unable to believe what a total prick he was. She walked up close to him and kicked him in the bollocks. It felt good to kick him there, where it was warm and soft. He went down, doubled up, gasping for breath. She kicked him in the face and he curled up into a ball. He covered his face with his hands. She kicked him in the face again, in the gut, in the back, then she stamped on his head. She was panting with the effort, her hair wild about her face. Her skin gleaming with sweat. She stopped and took a deep breath. Calm down. Calm down, Marie. She took the whiskey bottle and glugged at it, then she spat some of the whiskey over The Man. She paused to collect her thoughts. She was done. It was over. She picked up her bag and put on her coat. She went over to his suit jacket and took out his wallet. She emptied out the money and pocketed it. The Man had got up now. He was crouched on the floor, holding his stomach and watching her.

She stared at him for a long time, until his discomfort was visible.

It was the last thing she gave me, she said.

I'm sorry?

The doll.

Oh, I see.

The night before she died. She gave me that doll. It's the only thing I had of her.

I'm so sorry. Really, I am.

No you're not.

I am. I had no idea it meant so much to you. I just thought it was a bit of rubbish.

I used to lie holding it for months after she died. I used to talk to it like it was mum. Somehow, that doll, was a link. The one thing I could touch that was mum.

I'm really sorry. I'd get it back for you, but it will have gone to where ever they take it all to.

They take it to a landfill site.

Do they? I didn't know that.

You could get it if you really wanted to.

That's a ridiculous suggestion. I mean, it would be like looking for a needle in a haystack.

You could look. It's there. That means it can be found.

Well, I mean, I would do, but...

But you don't care.

I do. I do really. I'd go now if I could, but it's dark. There's no way I could see anything.

You could go tomorrow, when it's light. But you won't, because, despite what you say, the only reason you want me here is because you—

That just isn't true, Maria. I promise you. I'll tell you what. I'll book some time off tomorrow. They owe me some time back.

Go and get it.

I would, but, it's dark now. There's no way I can find it. I'll get it for you tomorrow.

Too late... I'm going.

Where are you going?

That's none of your fucking business is it? Eh?

I don't suppose it is, no. It's just that I'm worried about you.

She fastened her coat. It was a bit late for his worry now. She went towards the door.

The pass, she said, and held out her hand.

He took the key pass out of his pocket and handed it to her. She put it in the door and it opened.

Maria?

What?

Please. You don't have to go. Stay here. I'll do anything for you if you stay.

She thought about it for a moment but then shook her head. She closed the door behind her. She was gone.

He stared at the closed door, willing her back. He stared at the oblong of wood and paint. He stared at the lines around the door. The black lines where there was no light. He walked around the flat, which now contained just one person. Again. He walked around the chair where he had pushed The Girl, heady with wine, and around the table, where he had served her supper. He walked to the window where they had stood and watched the lights from the buildings and streets. The white and yellow lights. And the blackness in between the lights. He walked to the wall and banged his head against it. His head thumped with the dull pain. He banged it again. This time the pain was sharp and crisp. He banged it again, and again. Until, finally, he collapsed on the cushions and wept.

7

The first day she left he rang in sick. He lay in bed and stared at the ceiling. The second day he got out of bed and boiled an egg. He filled a glass with water. He sat at the table and stared at his plate. He had no appetite. He took a sip of the water. He could manage a sip of the water. He collapsed on the floor and stared at the wall. On the third day his alarm woke him up at the usual time but once again, he couldn't face the day, and he lay on his back for hours until it was dark again, only getting up to go to the toilet. After a week of moping round the flat, his boss rang him up. He wanted to know the reason for his absence. He explained that he had a virus. He didn't want to tell his boss he was depressed. His boss would have just said something like, snap out of it, or, pull yourself together, man.

He couldn't snap out of it. He couldn't pull himself together. After two weeks he went to the doctors and was prescribed some anti-depressants. They took the edge off it, but he still felt hollowed out. He still felt like the blood in his veins had been replaced with lead. He got in his car and drove to the coast. He sat on the beach and watched the waves. He watched the tide come in. He watched the tide go out. He booked into a bed and breakfast. He managed to eat some chips.

When he got home there were messages on his answer phone from his boss. He knew he wasn't coping. He hadn't got dressed since he'd returned to the flat, just moped about in his underwear. His appetite had returned but he had no enthusiasm for cooking. The apartment was strewn with empty bottles and take-away packaging. There were piles of crumpled clothes on the floor. He hadn't bathed for days. He was oblivious to his own funk.

He paced the room. He went over to the window. He stared out at the city below. He went over to the television and switched it on. He collapsed on the cushions and used the remote to switch through the channels. He switched all the way through, then started again. He did this several times, before eventually switching the television off. He stared at the black screen and at his own dark reflection framed within. He paced the room again. He went over to the window again. He picked up a magazine and flicked through the pages, before putting it back on the floor. He collapsed in the corner.

During the first week he had held up some hope that she would return, but now it had finally sunk in: she was not coming back. That was it.

The Girl had gone back to the street. She'd returned to a squat she and a few others were using – an empty house that still had running water. She'd lived in worse places. She'd dossed in doorways, in parks and under bridges. She'd slept under the tarpaulin of a boat that had been parked in a driveway. Another time she had slept in a garden shed that was falling down around her.

The first week she had come back from the flat she had lived like a queen. She had bought beers for everyone and spirits. She had ordered pizzas and other take-away meals. But the three hundred pounds she'd taken from his wallet was soon spent and then she was back to where she was before.

Why don't you get some more money off the cunt? one of her friends had said. It was a reasonable question. But the strange thing was, as she stood by the window and looked out across the city, it wasn't money she was thinking about. It was dark outside, but it was darker inside. These people weren't her friends. Who was she kidding? They were just a bunch of desperados, pretending to be friends, so that they felt less alone, but they were no more together than The Man. Despite there being more of them, they were no less lonely. She was no less lonely. They had used her for the money she had stolen from The Man but now that the money was spent she was just another rat crawling in the shit. If they'd found her dead in the morning, they would have raided her pockets and dibbed her clothes. Fought over who got her trainers, who got her coat. She pulled her beanie over her head and left them in the other room. They were smoking and drinking, but she didn't want anything from them.

The Man was in his corner. He was ripping pages out of a magazine and scrunching them into a ball. He threw them at the wastepaper bin, but he missed every time. Eventually he gave up – he put his head in his hands. He heard the door open and he looked up. It was The Girl.

You've come back?

The Girl smiled sarcastically, Yep.

I thought I'd lost you. Three weeks. I've thought about nothing else. I've been off work sick. World of Carpets. That's what they've got me doing.

World of Carpets. I couldn't focus on it. I just kept thinking of you on your own. Nowhere to live. No one to look after you. I've been back to that place looking for you every night. How've you been coping?

The Girl sat down on the swinging chair. She looked around the room. What a shit hole. Even worse than the one she had just left. But it could all get tidied up. She would put him to work. He needed someone to tell him what to do. Without that he was lost.

Alright.

Have you been stealing again?

What's it got to do with you?

He wasn't judging her. It was just that he was concerned. You can get into a lot of trouble.

I'm thirsty.

Ok, that's not a problem. What would you like? Tea, coffee, beer, wine?

I'll have a beer.

He went to the fridge and took out two ice cold Peronis. He didn't bother with glasses. The Girl guzzled from the bottle he handed to her.

Are you staying the night or is it just a passing visit?

We'll see.

Oh, right. That sounds fair.

It all depends.

Does it? Really? What on?

On you.

Right. Well. That's a plan then.

I'm hungry.

I'll make you some supper. What do you fancy?

Bring me that recipe book over there.

The Man fetched the book and The Girl leafed through its pages. She liked the glossy photographs. She pointed to one at random.

I'll have that.

Let me see. Oh, good choice. That's a tapenade of black olives and anchovies.

She flicked through again until she came to another glossy photograph that she liked the look of. She pointed at it.

Spiced prawns. I think there's prawns in the freezer. I'll have to check.

She turned the page and pointed again.

Marinated squid, with chickpeas. I've actually ran out of squid. I could do you that one, he said, pointing to a similar dish. You fry it in a hot griddle. It's just as good. Better if anything.

In fact, he'd run out of a lot of the ingredients, but he could substitute, she wouldn't notice. He still had a lot of things in the freezer.

I suppose so.

Anything else?

That should do it... Tell you what, you can put some music on.

What sort of thing are you into?

Machine.

I see.

He stood there clutching the book and nodding with a gormless smile on his face.

You don't know what Machine is, do you?

I do. It's a band, right?

It's a style of music.

Oh, that Machine. I thought you meant the band Machine.

The Girl smiled, in fact she'd made it up. There was no band or genre of music by that name that she knew of.

How's the beer?

Not bad.

Great.

Ok, I admit it, I've never heard of Machine. What is it?

It's a type of punk music.

I see.

His heart sunk. He hated punk music. Why make something sound so discordant? Surely music was there to sooth and delight the ear, not assault it.

I can play some Machine if you like.

Have you got some?

Well, no... I've got the last Kate Bush album. Have you heard that?

No.

It's very good. Would you like to?

No.

151

So music is perhaps not our thing... The same music. Well, different music. Not to worry. I'm sure there are plenty of other things we've got in common.

He opened his laptop and searched for 'machine' but it didn't bring anything up. The Girl went into his Spotify account and selected some music. She turned it up so that it was loud. She enjoyed watching The Man's discomfort.

The Man was trying to stay open minded. He wanted to be open to new sounds. He gritted his teeth and tensed the muscles down his spine but after two minutes of listening to the noise, it was a torture he could no longer stand. He clicked the pause button.

Put that track back on.

He did but turned the sound down at the same time.

Most of what you listen to is shit.

Really? Do you think so?

Annie Lennox, Gloria Estefan, Eric Clapton, Paul Simon, Sting.

Well, actually, Sting is a really gifted musician.

He's a wanker.

Yes, well, I suppose as a collection of music, it is a bit out of date. That's the great thing about Spotify. I hardly buy music these days...

I wouldn't really call what you listen to music.

Really? Would you not? What would you call it then?

Wallpaper... if I was being polite... dogwank, if I was being honest.

He didn't like having his musical tastes dismissed, but he had let himself get out of touch with the latest sounds.

Are you ready for that bit of supper?

I want you to do something first.

Oh really? What's that?

I want you to get me my doll back.

But Maria, it's been three weeks now. I mean, there's very little chance-

You either go and get it or I walk out and never come back.

But it's nearly midnight.

It's your choice, if you don't go, I won't stay. It's up to you.

It was insane, he knew it, but after some moments he found himself digging out an old coat from the bottom of the wardrobe and a powerful torch. He walked back in the room. She was watching television and drinking beer, swinging in the spherical chair. He told her he would be some time and she said that she wouldn't wait up for him. And he went to the door.

Outside it was cold and wet and dark. He walked to the back of the apartment to the enclosed area where the waste was kept in skips, ready for the council to collect it. The gates were locked and he had to walk around the periphery until he came to a part of the fence that he could climb over. As he began to wade through the refuse, he almost gagged on the stench.

The torch illuminated a small area. He watched as night insects tried to dodge the raindrops. Woodlice, millipedes and hundreds of slimy, crawly things he could not put a name to. He tried to focus on the task at hand. He would only search the first few skips, he decided. That's where the recent refuse would be. And at least then, he wouldn't have to wade through the worst of the decay.

But then he thought, it's been three weeks. Perhaps I need to start further back. He tried to imagine what the size of three weeks' worth of refuse would look like. About this much he decided and climbed the mound of filth further on. There were black bags piled onto black bags. There were rats scurrying over the top. There were slugs clinging to the plastic. The rain was coming down in buckets now. The colours were muted in this light. Everything looked grey or black. He tore at the black plastic to reveal the contents.

Cardboard, bottles, cans, old clothes. Decomposing vegetation: rotting salads, sprouting potatoes, mouldy tomatoes. He groped through the grease and worm juice. He delved into the steaming pile of offal and compost. He gagged. He wretched out some watery vomit. He pulled his collar over his mouth and nose and used the fabric to shield him from the vilest stenches. He moved onto the next bag: mouldy old teabags, rotting meat, soiled nappies. Discarded tissues.

It was hopeless. He knew that. But he had to at least try. He had to do his best to find it even though he knew there was no way of finding it. He moved to another bag, renewed his effort, sifting through the shit: tampons, plastic bottles, tin foil trays, Styrofoam cups, used condoms. All the debris and detritus of human life.

8

It was morning when he returned. Maria was sitting at the dining table when he walked in. She looked up at him. He was stained with refuse and soaking from the rain. She could smell his vile odour from where she was sitting.

Did you get it?

Oh, you're up. I thought you'd still be in bed.

It's ten o'clock. I've been up for nearly an hour. I'm waiting for my breakfast... where's my doll?

I looked everywhere, Maria. There's just so much of it. Then it started raining. I tried my best.

You failed?

I'm afraid so... Sorry. I need to get cleaned up. I'm going to have a shower I think.

Breakfast.

I'll fix something up once I've got cleaned. Is that ok?

Well, in fact, that's not ok. It's ten o'clock. I've been up since nine. I need something to eat. Just wash your hands. You can have a shower later.

What do you want?

Fried egg, make sure the yoke is still runny, two rashers of bacon, sausages, fried bread and a couple of rounds of toast.

Tea or coffee?

Both.

Right, well I'd best crack on then.

He went over to the kitchen area and rolled up his sleeves. He washed his hands, then took out some of the ingredients from the fridge and started to prepare breakfast.

When are you going back to work?

Well, the doctor's signed me off for another week.

What for? There's nothing wrong with you?

Well, physically not, no. I've been diagnosed with depression. The medication is kicking in now though and I'm feeling a bit better.

Good. I've been thinking about Mark Simpson.

Really? In what way?

Tell me about World of Carpets?

Well, I'm convinced that's one of the main problems. Having to watch my back all the time. All kinds of office battles going on.

Fine. It's nothing we can't sort.

Really? Do you think so?

Yep.

Fantastic.

I don't think there's anything wrong with your ideas, Steve. The problem is this Simpson cock. And that's what we're going to sort out after breakfast.

Right. Well, I best crack on then.

He took an egg and cracked it into the pan. He smiled at his own joke and started to whistle a tune.

The Girl opened the morning paper and flicked through it. She turned to her horoscope. Today will provide new opportunities, she read. She started to giggle.

9

The Girl was swinging in the chair wearing just a silk robe. She had a box of chocolates on her lap and a glass of wine in her hand. She was watching television when The Man walked in wearing a suit and carrying a briefcase.

I'm home.

So how did it go?

He took off his jacket and searched for a hanger to put it away neatly.

Can I have some of that? he said, pointing to the bottle.

Sure, get a glass.

He returned with a glass and The Girl poured him a small portion. She turned off the television.

So go on.

He loosened his tie and lay down on the cushions.

The boss had Mark in the office for an hour today. I couldn't hear what he was saying but he was doing a lot of shouting. I could see from the window that he was red in the face and he was pointing at him. Like this.

The Man did his impression of the boss.

Then Mark comes out looking really sheepish. Doesn't look up, just walks back to his desk and slumps in his chair.

What did I tell you?

It gets better. About half an hour later, the boss invites me in. He's had the caterers in. So there we are, laughing and eating sandwiches. And then right, three o'clock comes and he says, right Steve, I'm taking you for a drink, you've earned it.

What about World of Carpets.

You were right. He'd given that to Mark.

Ha!

It gets even better.

Go on.

Well, when we get to the pub, we order a few pints, get sat down, and he only goes and offers me Calvin Klein. Bloody Calvin Klein. Can you believe it!

You see?

Like clockwork. Everything you said. How did you know?

It's just fucking obvious.

The Man laughed out of sheer joy. He couldn't believe how wonderful The Girl was.

Have you eaten?

Yes, I got a takeaway when I knew you were going to be late.

Good, I've eaten too. He insisted on buying me supper at the pub – to clinch the deal. I'm exhausted actually. It's been a very long day. Thought I'd drink this and crash out.

Well, there's a film on later I want to watch.

It was ok. He would put his earplugs in. He was getting used to sleeping on the floor now with The Girl watching the television. He'd slept rather well last night.

Don't suppose there's any chance of you changing your mind?

What about?

About me moving in with you. It's a big bed. I wouldn't touch you or anything. I'd wear pyjamas.

We'll see.

Really?

Best not to rush things.

She was right, of course. He could wait. It would be worth it in the end.

There is something I wanted to ask you, he said.

Go on?

Well, while I was waiting for the tube, I was reading one of those magazines you read, you know, True Crimes. Here, I'll show you.

He got up and went over to his briefcase. He took out a magazine.

There's this story. And it's about this serial killer.

It's a True Crimes magazine, Steve. What do you expect? Stories about rescuing kittens?

The thing is, it interviews the child of one of the victims. I say child, he's now grown up. Richard he's called. And he tells about the night of the attack. About waiting at the bus stop for his mum to come home. He's written a book and it's all in there. About her body being found just a few feet away from the bus stop, all of it. Now how about that for a coincidence?

The Girl was momentarily stuck for words.

Have you been lying to me, Maria?

She quickly composed herself.

You don't understand.

What?

I didn't want to tell you.

Tell me what?

I'm in hiding.

I know about that.

Not just from the police though.

What?

Richard is me. My pen name. I had to... my family ... they're a bunch of psychos. If they'd seen my name on a book, don't you think they would have read it?

Fucking hell, Maria. You must think I'm stupid. And I am not stupid. I'm in advertising, for fuck's sake. I wasn't dossing in a doorway, or nicking stuff from a distracted dogging party. I've got a respectable job... So don't, don't, don't try and pull the wool over my eyes – it won't wash. I'll not be lied to. Now I want the truth.

I will tell you the truth, but you've got to promise me one thing.

What?

You've got to believe me this time.

Why should I?

Because, I'm trusting you with my life. Don't you see, if this gets out, both our lives are at risk.

What are you talking about?

Everything I've told you is true. The book was written as a novel by a ghost writer. That's who Richard is. It was an agent who took up my story, and put me together with Richard. He interviewed me for weeks, months even. He recorded it all on a machine and every night he'd write up the entire conversation. In the morning we'd go over the printout together, and in the afternoon, I'd tell him the next chapter. We couldn't risk putting my name to it.

Why not?

My dad. That's why not. I've told you. He's Irish traveller. He's a pikey. They put contracts out on you. They kill you for bringing dishonour on the family.

Are you sure about this?

Listen. Despite all the things the publishers did to protect me. My dad found out. There's a contract on me now. That's why I'm in hiding. If they find me, they'll kill me. You've saved my life, and I'll always be grateful for that.

How do I know you're telling the truth?

You promised me you'd believe me.

But, but...

Do you really think I'd make it up?

So why didn't you just tell me?

I wasn't sure. I just wasn't sure what you'd do. I didn't want to put your life in danger. I didn't want to scare you. I know you're under a lot of pressure at work, and I didn't know how to break it to you. I was torn.

I see.

Actually, it's a big relief. I'm so glad, finally, to clear it up. Why don't we celebrate? Open a bottle of champagne. You've got a massive contract. You should be relaxing and having a good time.

He was partly tempted but he'd already had enough to drink.

Anyway, what about you. You're a fine one to talk, The Girl said.

What do you mean?

That night you found me, pretending you didn't know what was going on.

Please, Maria, I'm not like that. I had no idea that sort of thing went on, even.

So why were you there?

I've told you, I fancied a drive.

But you weren't driving, you were parked up, in a car park full of doggers. Bit suspicious don't you think.

I could say the same about you.

I think I made it clear. I was stealing. I got caught. I had nothing to do with those perverts.

No, of course not. I'm sorry. I'm not suggesting you were.

Just because you're one of them, don't tar me with your brush.

But, look, really, I had nothing to do with it.

He looked at her imploringly. She shook her head.

Ok, I'll tell you the truth.... I went there for a reason. Yes. You were right about that. But it wasn't for the reason you think. I really had no idea it was a popular spot for, you know what.

Dogging.

Precisely. I'd been there for nearly an hour, before those cars came and started, well, you know what I mean.

Having a picnic?

Well, something like that.

So why were you there?

I was there because... I had a rubber hose... I went there to kill myself. Ok? I wanted to die. That was my reason for being there.

What?

I, I wanted to do myself in. I was psyching myself up. I had an Enya CD. I was going to float into that ocean of sound. I was going to sink into the Caribbean Blue. I just wanted to end it all.

Why didn't you?

Because I saw you. I saw the trouble you were in. I wanted to help you. It put it all in perspective. I mean, it made me reflect on my own life. It was a moment, just a moment, when everything made sense. I saw my whole life, and, and I realised I had a mission, and that mission was you.

So *I* saved *you*?

Yes.

I saved your life.

The Girl laughed.

It's not the first time.

You've tried to kill yourself before you mean?

Yes. With pills. I was working late. I was on my own. I thought I was on my own. There was a cleaner. She found me. She rang nine nine nine.

He closed his eyes and saw himself waking up in a hospital, in a hospital bed, in a hospital gown, with hospital lights all around him.

Do you believe me?

The Girl stroked his hair, Course I do, she said, Now lie back.

He did as he was told. She told him to close his eyes and he did this as well. She continued to stroke his hair and told him to relax. She stroked his hair some more and told him to go to sleep. He could feel himself slipping into unconsciousness, that glorious feeling between two worlds. He was aware of The Girl stroking his hair, over and over. Then she said

160

to him, Go to sleep.

I love you, Maria.

I know you do, Steve. Now you've got a busy day tomorrow, you need to get some sleep. Ssshhh.

She stroked his hair gently until his breathing became heavy and she knew he was asleep. Very slowly, careful not to wake him, she freed herself from the weight of his body and lay him on the cushions. She went over to the fridge and took out a bottle of white. She hadn't cared for his choice of wine at first, it wasn't sweet enough, but she was acquiring the taste for it now. It was funny that, the things from her childhood that she had liked, she didn't like now. And the things she didn't like, they had become the things she liked. The things you don't like become the things you like the most.

And she thought about this some more as she sipped from the glass. She reached into the pocket of her robe and pulled out the doll. She held it up and looked into its eyes. Two black crosses, hand stitched. Black wool hair tied in pig tails. This was the only thing she had left now to remind her of what she had been. It was enough. The doll represented the past, and now it was about her future.

She went over to the window and peered down at the city. She looked at the bright lights below, laid out like a box of jewels. White lights and yellow lights, silver and gold, how they shimmered and glittered. But between the lights there was nothing at all.

162

Acknowledgements

Many thanks to the following readers and writers for kindly
offering editorial assistance and expertise: Simon Crump,
Steve Ely, Jim Greenhalf, and Matt Hill.

164

About the author

Michael Stewart is a multi-award-winning writer for radio, TV and theatre, a novelist and a short-story writer. His novels include King Crow and Ill Will: The Untold Story of Heathcliff. He is Head of Creative Writing at the University of Huddersfield and editor of Grist Books. He is also the creator of the Brontë Stones project, four monumental stones situated in the landscape between the birthplace and the parsonage, inscribed with poems by Kate Bush, Carol Ann Duffy, Jeannette Winterson and Jackie Kay.